The vision of Earth dwindling and retreating is an awesome symbol, equivalent to eternal loss, to the act of dying itself. The more impressionable cadets could not look astern without finding their eyes swimming with tears. Even the suave Culpepper was awed by the magnificence of the spectacle, the sun an aching pit not to be tolerated, Earth a plump pearl rolling on black velvet among a myriad of glittering diamonds. And away from Earth, away from the sun, opened an exalted magnificence of another order entirely.

For the first time the cadets became dimly aware that Henry Belt had spoken truly of strange visions. Here was death, here was peace, solitude, star-blazing beauty which promised not oblivion in death but eternity. . . . Streams and spatters of stars. . . . The familiar constellations, the stars with their prideful names presenting themselves like heroes: Achernar, Fomalhaut, Sadal, Suud, Canopus. . . .

HENRY BELT

DUST
OF
FAR SUNS

Jack Vance

Formerly titled: *Future Tense*

DAW BOOKS, INC.
DONALD A. WOLLHEIM, PUBLISHER

1633 Broadway, New York, NY 10019

PUBLISHED BY
THE NEW AMERICAN LIBRARY
OF CANADA LIMITED

Copyright ©, 1964, by Jack Vance.

All Rights Reserved.

Cover art by Paul Chadwick.

ACKNOWLEDGMENTS:

The Gift of Gab, © 1955, by Street & Smith Publications, Inc.
Dust of Far Suns, © 1962, as *Sail 25,* by Ziff-Davis Publishing Co. *Ullward's Retreat,* © 1958, by Galaxy Publishing Corp. *Dodkin's Job,* © 1959, by Street & Smith Publications, Inc. By arrangement with the author.

FIRST DAW PRINTING, JANUARY 1981

1 2 3 4 5 6 7 8 9

DAW TRADEMARK REGISTERED
U.S. PAT. OFF. MARCA
REGISTRADA. HECHO EN U.S.A.

PRINTED IN CANADA
COVER PRINTED IN U.S.A.

Table of Contents

DUST OF FAR SUNS

Chapter 1

Henry Belt came limping into the conference room, mounted the dais, settled himself at the desk. He looked once around the room: a swift bright glance which, focusing nowhere, treated the eight young men who faced him to an almost insulting disinterest. He reached in his pocket, brought forth a pencil and a flat red book, which he placed on the desk. The eight young men watched in absolute silence. They were much alike: healthy, clean, smart, their expressions identically alert and wary. Each had heard legends of Henry Belt, each had formed his private plans and private determinations.

Henry Belt seemed a man of a different species. His face was broad, flat, roped with cartilage and muscle, with skin the color and texture of bacon rind. Coarse white grizzle covered his scalp, his eyes were crafty slits, his nose a misshapen lump. His shoulders were massive, his legs short and gnarled.

"First of all," said Henry Belt, with a gap-toothed grin, "I'll make it clear that I don't expect you to like me. If you do I'll be surprised and displeased. It will mean that I haven't pushed you hard enough."

He leaned back in his chair, surveyed the silent group. "You've heard stories about me. Why haven't they kicked me out of the service? Incorrigible, arrogant, dangerous

Henry Belt. Drunken Henry Belt. (This last of course is slander. Henry Belt has never been drunk in his life.) Why do they tolerate me? For one simple reason: out of necessity. No one wants to take on this kind of job. Only a man like Henry Belt can stand up to it: year after year in space, with nothing to look at but a half-dozen round-faced young scrubs. He takes them out, he brings them back. Not all of them, and not all of those who come back are spacemen today. But they'll all cross the street when they see him coming. Henry Belt? you say. They'll turn pale or go red. None of them will smile. Some of them are high-placed now. They could kick me loose if they chose. Ask them why they don't. Henry Belt is a terror, they'll tell you. He's wicked, he's a tyrant. Cruel as an axe, fickle as a woman. But a voyage with Henry Belt blows the foam off the beer. He's ruined many a man, he's killed a few, but those that come out of it are proud to say, I trained with Henry Belt!

"Another thing you may hear: Henry Belt has luck. But don't pay any heed. Luck runs out. You'll be my thirteenth class, and that's unlucky. I've taken out seventy-two young sprats, no different from yourselves; I've come back twelve times: which is partly Henry Belt and partly luck. The voyages average about two years long: how can a man stand it? There's only one who could: Henry Belt. I've got more space-time than any man alive, and now I'll tell you a secret: this is my last time out. I'm starting to wake up at night to strange visions. After this class I'll quit. I hope you lads aren't superstitious. A white-eyed woman told me that I'd die in space. She told me other things and they've all come true. We'll get to know each other well. And you'll be wondering on what basis I make my recommendations. Am I objective and fair? Do I put aside personal animosity? Naturally there won't be any friendship. Well, here's my system. I keep a red book. Here it is. I'll put your names down right now. You, sir?"

"I'm Cadet Lewis Lynch, sir."

"You?"

"Edward Culpepper, sir."

"Marcus Verona, sir."

8

"Vidal Weske, sir."

"Marvin McGrath, sir."

"Barry Ostrander, sir."

"Clyde von Gluck, sir."

"Joseph Sutton, sir."

Henry Belt wrote the names in the red book. "This is the system. When you do something to annoy me, I mark you down demerits. At the end of the voyage I total these demerits, add a few here and there for luck, and am so guided. I'm sure nothing could be clearer than this. What annoys me? Ah, that's a question which is hard to answer. If you talk too much: demerits. If you're surly and taciturn: demerits. If you slouch and laze and dog the dirty work: demerits. If you're overzealous and forever scuttling about: demerits. Obsequiousness: demerits. Truculence: demerits. If you sing and whistle: demerits. If you're a stolid bloody bore: demerits. You can see that the line is hard to draw. Here's a hint which can save you many marks. I don't like gossip, especially when it concerns myself. I'm a sensitive man, and I open my red book fast when I think I'm being insulted." Henry Belt once more leaned back in his chair. "Any questions?"

No one spoke.

Henry Belt nodded. "Wise. Best not to flaunt your ignorance so early in the game. In response to the thought passing through each of your skulls, I do not think of myself as God. But you may do so, if you choose. And this—" he held up the red book "—you may regard as the Syncretic Compendium. Very well. Any questions?"

"Yes, sir," said Culpepper.

"Speak, sir."

"Any objection to alcoholic beverages aboard ship, sir?"

"For the cadets, yes indeed. I concede that the water must be carried in any event, that the organic compounds present may be reconstituted, but unluckily the bottles weigh far too much."

"I understand, sir."

Henry Belt rose to his feet. "One last word. Have I mentioned that I run a tight ship? When I say jump, I expect everyone of you to jump. This is dangerous work, of course. I don't guarantee your safety. Far from it, especially since we are assigned to old 25, which should have been broken up long ago. There are eight of you present. Only six cadets will make the voyage. Before the week is over I will make the appropriate notifications. Any more questions? . . . Very well, then. Cheerio." Limping on his thin legs as if his feet hurt, Henry Belt departed into the back passage.

For a moment or two there was silence. Then von Gluck said in a soft voice, "My gracious."

"He's a tyrannical lunatic," grumbled Weske. "I've never heard anything like it! Megalomania!"

"Easy," said Culpepper. "Remember, no gossiping."

"Bah!" muttered McGrath. "This is a free country. I'll damn well say what I like."

Weske rose to his feet. "A wonder somebody hasn't killed him."

"I wouldn't want to try it," said Culpepper. "He looks tough." He made a gesture, stood up, brow furrowed in thought. Then he went to look along the passageway into which Henry Belt had made his departure. There, pressed to the wall, stood Henry Belt. "Yes, sir," said Culpepper suavely. "I forgot to inquire when you wanted us to convene again."

Henry Belt returned to the rostrum. "Now is as good a time as any." He took his seat, opened his red book. "You, Mr. von Gluck, made the remark, 'My gracious' in an offensive tone of voice. One demerit. You, Mr. Weske, employed the terms 'tyrannical lunatic' and 'megalomania' in reference to myself. Three demerits. Mr. McGrath, you observed that freedom of speech is the official doctrine of this country. It is a theory which right now we have no time to explore, but I believe that the statement in its present context carries an overtone of insubordination. One demerit, Mr. Culpepper, your imperturbable complacence irritates me. I prefer that you display more uncertainty, or even uneasiness."

"Sorry, sir."

"However, you took occasion to remind your colleagues of my rule, and so I will not mark you down."

10

"Thank you, sir."

Henry Belt leaned back in the chair, stared at the ceiling. "Listen closely, as I do not care to repeat myself. Take notes if you wish. Topic: Solar Sails, Theory and Practice thereof. Material with which you should already be familiar, but which I will repeat in order to avoid ambiguity.

"First, why bother with the sail, when nuclear-jet ships are faster, more dependable, more direct, safer, and easier to navigate? The answer is three-fold. First, a sail is not a bad way to move heavy cargo slowly but cheaply through space. Secondly, the range of the sail is unlimited, since we employ the mechanical pressure of light for thrust, and therefore need carry neither propulsive machinery, material to be ejected, nor energy source. The solar sail is much lighter than its nuclear-powered counterpart, and may carry a larger complement of men in a larger hull. Thirdly, to train a man for space there is no better instrument than the handling of a sail. The computer naturally calculates sail cant and plots the course; in fact, without the computer we'd be dead ducks. Nevertheless the control of a sail provides working familiarity with the cosmic elementals: light, gravity, mass, space.

"There are two types of sail: pure and composite. The first relies on solar energy exclusively, the second carries a secondary power source. We have been assigned Number 25, which is the first sort. It consists of a hull, a large parabolic reflector which serves as radar and radio antenna, as well as reflector for the power generator; and the sail itself. The pressure of radiation, of course, is extremely slight—on the order of an ounce per acre at this distance from the sun. Necessarily the sail must be extremely large and extremely light. We use a fluoro-siliconic film a tenth of a mil in gauge, fogged with lithium to the state of opacity. I believe the layer of lithium is about a thousand two hundred molecules thick. Such a foil weighs about four tons to the square mile. It is fitted to a hoop of thin-walled tubing, from which mono-crystalline iron cords lead to the hull.

"We try to achieve a weight factor of six tons to the square mile, which produces an acceleration of between

11

g/100 and g/1000 depending on proximity to the sun, angle of cant, circumsolar orbital speed, reflectivity of surface. These accelerations seem minute, but calculation shows them to be cumulatively enormous. G/100 yields a velocity increment of 800 miles per hour every hour, 18,-000 miles per hour each day, or five miles per second each day. At this rate interplanetary distances are readily negotiable—with proper manipulation of the sail, I need hardly say.

"The virtues of the sail, I've mentioned. It is cheap to build and cheap to operate. It requires neither fuel nor ejectant. As it travels through space, the great area captures various ions, which may be expelled in the plasma jet powered by the parabolic reflector, which adds another increment to the acceleration.

"The disadvantages of the sail are those of the glider or sailing ship, in that we must use natural forces with great precision and delicacy.

"There is no particular limit to the size of the sail. On 25 we use about four square miles of sail. For the present voyage we will install a new sail, as the old is well-worn and eroded.

"That will be all for today." Once more Henry Belt limped down from the dais and out the passage. On this occasion there were no comments.

Chapter 2

★   ★   ★

The eight cadets shared a dormitory, attended classes together, ate at the same table in the mess hall. In various shops and laboratories they assembled, disassembled—and reassembled computers, pumps, generators, gyro-platforms, star-trackers, communication gear. "It's not enough to be clever with your hands," said Henry Belt. "Dexterity is not enough. Resourcefulness, creativity, the ability to make successful improvisations—these are more important. We'll test you out." And presently each of the cadets was introduced into a room on the floor of which lay a great heap of mingled housings, wires, flexes, gears, components of a dozen varieties of mechanism. "This is a twenty-six-hour test," said Henry Belt. "Each of you has an identical set of components and supplies. There shall be no exchange of parts or information between you. Those whom I suspect of this fault will be dropped from the class, without recommendation. What I want you to build is, first, one standard Aminex Mark 9 Computer. Second, a servo-mechanism to orient a mass ten kilograms toward Mu Hercules. Why Mu Hercules?"

"Because, sir, the solar system moves in the direction of Mu Hercules, and we thereby avoid parallax error. Negligible though it may be, sir."

"The final comment smacks of frivolity, Mr. McGrath, which serves only to distract the attention of those who are trying to take careful notes of my instructions. One demerit."

"Sorry, sir. I merely intended to express my awareness that for many practical purposes such a degree of accuracy is unnecessary."

"That idea, cadet, is sufficiently elemental that it need not be labored. I appreciate brevity and precision."

"Yes, sir."

"Thirdly, from these materials, assemble a communication system, operating on one hundred watts, which will permit two-way conversation between Tycho Base and Phobos, at whatever frequency you deem suitable."

The cadets started in identical fashion by sorting the material into various piles, then calibrating and checking the test instruments. Achievement thereafter was disparate. Culpepper and von Gluck, diagnosing the test as partly one of mechanical ingenuity and partly ordeal by frustration, failed to become excited when several indispensable components proved either to be missing or inop-

13

erative, and carried each project as far as immediately feasible. McGrath and Weske, beginning with the computer, were reduced to rage and random action. Lynch and Sutton worked doggedly at the computer, Verona at the communication system.

Culpepper alone managed to complete one of the instruments, by the process of sawing, polishing and cementing together sections of two broken crystals into a crude, inefficient but operative maser unit.

The day after this test McGrath and Weske disappeared from the dormitory, whether by their own volition or notification from Henry Belt no one ever knew.

The test was followed by weekend leave. Cadet Lynch, attending a cocktail party, found himself in conversation with a Lieutenant-Colonel Trenchard, who shook his head pityingly to hear that Lynch was training with Henry Belt.

"I was up with Old Horrors myself. I tell you it's a miracle we ever got back. Belt was drunk two-thirds of the voyage."

"How does he escape court-martial?" asked Lynch.

"Very simple. All the top men seem to have trained under Henry Belt. Naturally they hate his guts but they all take a perverse pride in the fact. And maybe they hope that someday a cadet will take him apart."

"Has any ever tried?"

"Oh yes. I took a swing at Henry once. I was lucky to escape with a broken collarbone and two sprained ankles. If you come back alive, you'll stand a good chance of reaching the top."

The next evening Henry Belt passed the word. "Next Tuesday morning we go up. We'll be gone several months."

On Tuesday morning the cadets took their places in the angel-wagon. Henry Belt presently appeared. The pilot readied for takeoff.

"Hold your hats. On the count . . ." The projectile thrust against the earth, strained, rose, went streaking up into the sky. An hour later the pilot pointed. "There's

14

your boat. Old 25. And 39 right beside it, just in from space."

Henry Belt stared aghast from the port. "What's been done to the ship? The decoration? The red? the white? the yellow? The checkerboard."

"Thank some idiot of a landlubber," said the pilot. "The word came to pretty the old boats for a junket of congressmen."

Henry Belt turned to the cadets. "Observe this foolishness. It is the result of vanity and ignorance. We will be occupied several days removing the paint."

They drifted close below the two sails: No. 39 just down from space, spare and polished beside the bedizened structure of No. 25. In 39's exit port a group of men waited, their gear floating at the end of cords.

"Observe those men," said Henry Belt. "They are jaunty. They have been on a pleasant outing around the planet Mars. They are poorly trained. When you gentlemen return you will be haggard and desperate and well-trained. Now, gentlemen, clamp your helmets, and we will proceed."

The helmets were secured. Henry Belt's voice came by radio. "Lynch, Ostrander will remain here to discharge cargo. Verona, Culpepper, von Gluck, Sutton, leap with cords to the ship; ferry across the cargo, stow it in the proper hatches."

Henry Belt took charge of his personal cargo, which consisted of several large cases. He eased them out into space, clipped on lines, thrust them toward 25, leapt after. Pulling himself and the cases to the entrance port, he disappeared within.

Discharge of cargo was effected. The crew from 39 transferred to the carrier, which thereupon swung down and away, thrust itself dwindling back toward earth.

When the cargo had been stowed, the cadets gathered in the wardroom. Henry Belt appeared from the master's cubicle. "Gentlemen, how do you like the surroundings? Eh, Mr. Culpepper?"

"The hull is commodious, sir. The view is superb."

Henry Belt nodded. "Mr. Lynch? Your impressions?"

15

"I'm afraid I haven't sorted them out yet, sir."

"I see. You, Mr. Sutton?"

"Space is larger than I imagined it, sir."

"True. Space is unimaginable. A good spaceman must either be larger than space or he must ignore it. Both difficult. Well, gentlemen, I will make a few comments, then I will retire and enjoy the voyage. Since this is my last time out, I intend to do nothing whatever. The operation of the ship will be completely in your hands. I will merely appear from time to time to beam benevolently about or alas! to make remarks in my red book. Nominally I shall be in command, but you six will enjoy complete control over the ship. If you return as safely to Earth I will make an approving entry in my red book. If you wreck us or fling us into the sun, you will be more unhappy than I, since it is my destiny to die in space. Mr. von Gluck, do I perceive a smirk on your face?"

"No, sir, it is a thoughtful half-smile."

"What is humorous in the concept of my demise, may I ask?"

"It will be a great tragedy, sir. I merely was reflecting upon the contemporary persistence of, well, not exactly superstition, but, let us say, the conviction of a subjective cosmos."

Henry Belt made a notation in the red book. "Whatever is meant by this barbaric jargon I'm sure I don't know, Mr. von Gluck. It is clear that you fancy yourself a philosopher and dialectician. I will not fault this, so long as your remarks conceal no overtones of malice and insolence, to which I am extremely sensitive. Now as to the persistence of superstition, only an impoverished mind considers itself the repository of absolute knowledge. Hamlet spoke on the subject to Horatio, as I recall, in the well-known work by William Shakespeare. I myself have seen strange and terrifying sights. Were they hallucinations? Were they the manipulation of the cosmos by my mind or the mind of someone—or something—other than myself? I do not know. I therefore counsel a flexible attitude toward matters where the truth is still unknown. For this reason: the impact of an inexplicable experience may

16

well destroy a mind which is too brittle. Do I make myself clear?"

"Perfectly, sir."

"Very good. To return, then. We shall set a system of watches whereby each man works in turn with each of the other five. I thereby hope to discourage the formation of special friendships, or cliques."

"You have inspected the ship. The hull is a sandwich of lithium-beryllium, insulating foam, fiber, and an interior skin. Very light, held rigid by air pressure rather than by any innate strength of the material. We can therefore afford enough space to stretch our legs and provide all of us with privacy.

"The master's cubicle is to the left; under no circumstances is anyone permitted in my quarters. If you wish to speak to me, knock on my door. If I appear, good. If I do not appear, go away. To the right are six cubicles which you may now distribute among yourselves by lot.

"Your schedule will be two hours study, four hours on watch, six hours off. I will require no specific rate of study progress, but I recommend that you make good use of your time.

"Our destination is Mars. We will presently construct a new sail, then while orbital velocity builds up, you will carefully test and check all equipment aboard. Each of you will compute sail cant and course and work out among yourselves any discrepancies which may appear. I shall take no hand in navigation. I prefer that you involve me in no disaster. If any such occurs I shall severely mark down the persons responsible.

"Singing, whistling, humming, are forbidden. I disapprove of fear and hysteria, and mark accordingly. No one dies more than once; we are well aware of the risks of this, our chosen occupation. There will be no practical jokes. You may fight, so long as you do not disturb me or break any instruments; however, I counsel against it, as it leads to resentment, and I have known cadets to kill each other. I suggest coolness and detachment in your personal relations. Use of the microfilm projector is of course at your own option. You may not use the radio either to despatch or receive messages. In fact, I have put the radio

17

out of commission, as is my practice. I do this to emphasize the fact that, sink or swim, we must make do with our own resources. Are there any questions? . . . Very good. You will find that if you all behave with scrupulous correctness and accuracy, we shall in due course return safe and sound, with a minimum of demerits and no casualties. I am bound to say, however, that in twelve previous voyages this has failed to occur. Now you select your cubicles, stow your gear. The carrier will bring up the new sail tomorrow, and you will go to work."

Chapter 3

★ ★ ★

The carrier discharged a great bundle of three-inch tubing: paper-thin lithium hardened with beryllium, reinforced with filaments of mono-crystalline iron—a total length of eight miles. The cadets fitted the tubes end to end, cementing the joints. When the tube extended a quarter-mile it was bent bow-shaped by a cord stretched between two ends, and further sections added. As the process continued, the free end curved far out and around, and began to veer back in toward the hull. When the last tube was in place the loose end was hauled down, socketed home, to form a great hoop two and a half miles in diameter.

Henry Belt came out occasionally in his space suit to look on, and occasionally spoke a few words of sardonic comment, to which the cadets paid little heed. Their mood had changed; this was exhilaration, to be weightlessly afloat above the bright cloud-marked globe, with continent and ocean wheeling massively below. Anything seemed possible, even the training voyage with Henry

Belt! When he came out to inspect their work, they grinned at each other with indulgent amusement. Henry Belt suddenly seemed a rather pitiful creature, a poor vagabond suited only for drunken bluster. Fortunate indeed that they were less naive than Henry Belt's previous classes! They had taken Belt seriously; he had cowed them, reduced them to nervous pulp. Not this crew, not by a long shot! They saw through Henry Belt! Just keep your nose clean, do your work, keep cheerful. The training voyage won't last but a few months, and then real life begins. Gut it out, ignore Henry Belt as much as possible. This is the sensible attitude; the best way to keep on top of the situation.

Already the group had made a composite assessment of its members, arriving at a set of convenient labels. Culpepper: smooth, suave, easy-going. Lynch: excitable, argumentative, hot-tempered. Von Gluck: the artistic temperament, delicate with hands and sensibilities. Ostrander: prissy, finicky, over-tidy. Sutton: moody, suspicious, competitive. Verona: the plugger, rough at the edges, but persistent and reliable.

Around the hull swung the gleaming hoop, and now the carrier brought up the sail, a great roll of darkly shining stuff. When unfolded and unrolled, and unfolded many times more it became a tough, gleaming film, flimsy as gold leaf. Unfolded to its fullest extent it was a shimmering disk, already rippling and bulging to the light of the sun. The cadets fitted the film to the hoop, stretched it taut as a drumhead, cemented it in place. Now the sail must carefully be held edge on to the sun or it would quickly move away, under a thrust of about a hundred pounds.

From the rim braided-iron threads were led to a ring at the back of the parabolic reflector, dwarfing this as the reflector dwarfed the hull, and now the sail was ready to move.

The carrier brought up a final cargo: water, food, spare parts, a new magazine for the microfilm viewer, mail. Then Henry Belt said, "Make sail."

This was the process of turning the sail to catch the

19

sunlight while the hull moved around Earth away from the sun, canting it parallel to the sun rays when the ship moved on the sunward leg of its orbit; in short, building up an orbital velocity which in due course would stretch loose the bonds of terrestrial gravity and send Sail 25 kiting out toward Mars.

During this period the cadets checked every item of equipment aboard the vessel. They grimaced with disgust and dismay at some of the instruments: 25 was an old ship, with antiquated gear. Henry Belt seemed to enjoy their grumbling. "This is a training voyage, not a pleasure cruise. If you wanted your noses wiped, you should have taken a post on the ground. And, I have no sympathy for fault-finders. If you wish a model by which to form your own conduct, observe me."

The moody, introspective Sutton, usually the most diffident and laconic of individuals, ventured an ill-advised witticism. "If we modeled ourselves after you, sir, there'd be no room to move for the whisky."

Out came the red book. "Extraordinary impudence, Mr. Sutton. How can you yield so easily to malice?"

Sutton flushed pink; his eyes glistened, he opened his mouth to speak, then closed it firmly. Henry Belt, waiting, politely expectant, turned away. "You gentlemen will perceive that I rigorously obey my own rules of conduct. I am regular as a clock. There is no better, more genial shipmate than Henry Belt. There is not a fairer man alive. Mr. Culpepper, you have a remark to make?"

"Nothing of consequence, sir."

Henry Belt went to the port, glared out at the sail. He swung around instantly. "Who is on watch?"

"Sutton and Ostrander, sir."

"Gentlemen, have you noticed the sail? It has swung about and is canting to show its back to the sun. In another ten minutes we shall be tangled in a hundred miles of guy wires."

Sutton and Ostrander sprang to repair the situation. Henry Belt shook his head disparagingly. "This is precisely what is meant by the words 'negligence' and 'inattentiveness.' You two have committed a serious error.

20

This is poor spacemanship. The sail must always be in such a position as to hold the wires taut."

"There seems to be something wrong with the sensor, sir," Sutton blurted. "It should notify us when the sail swings behind us."

"I fear I must charge you an additional demerit for making excuses, Mr. Sutton. It is your duty to assure yourself that all the warning devices are functioning properly, at all times. Machinery must never be used as a substitute for vigilance."

Ostrander looked up from the control console. "Someone has turned off the switch, sir. I do not offer this as an excuse, but as an explanation."

"The line of distinction is often hard to define, Mr. Ostrander. Please bear in mind my remarks on the subject of vigilance."

"Yes, sir, but—who turned off the switch?"

"Both you and Mr. Sutton are theoretically hard at work watching for any such accident or occurrence. Did you not observe it?"

"No, sir."

"I almost accuse you of further inattention and neglect, in this case."

Ostrander gave Henry Belt a long dubious side-glance. "The only person I recall going near the console is yourself, sir. I'm sure you wouldn't do such a thing."

Henry Belt shook his head sadly. "In space you must never rely on anyone for rational conduct. A few moments ago Mr. Sutton unfairly imputed to me an unusual thirst for whisky. Suppose this were the case? Suppose, as an example of pure irony, that I had indeed been drinking whisky, that I was in fact drunk?"

"I will agree, sir, that anything is possible."

Henry Belt shook his head again. "That is the type of remark, Mr. Ostrander, that I have come to associate with Mr. Culpepper. A better response would have been, 'In the future, I will try to be ready for any conceivable contingency.' Mr. Sutton, did you make a hissing sound between your teeth?"

"I was breathing, sir."

"Please breathe with less vehemence."

21

Henry Belt turned away and wandered back and forth about the wardroom, scrutinizing cases, frowning at smudges on polished metal. Ostrander muttered something to Sutton, and both watched Henry Belt closely as he moved here and there. Presently Henry Belt lurched toward them. "You show great interest in my movements, gentlemen."

"We were on the watch for another unlikely contingency, sir."

"Very good, Mr. Ostrander. Stick with it. In space nothing is impossible. I'll vouch for this personally."

Chapter 4

★   ★   ★

Henry Belt sent all hands out to remove the paint from the surface of the parabolic reflector. When this had been accomplished, incident sunlight was focused upon an expanse of photoelectric cells. The power so generated was used to operate plasma jets, expelling ions collected by the vast expanse of sail, further accelerating the ship, thrusting it ever out into an orbit of escape. And finally one day, at an exact instant dictated by the computer, the ship departed from Earth and floated tangentially out into space, off at an angle for the orbit of Mars. At an acceleration of g/100 velocity built up rapidly. Earth dwindled behind; the ship was isolated in space. The cadets' exhilaration vanished, to be replaced by an almost funereal solemnity. The vision of Earth dwindling and retreating is an awesome symbol, equivalent to eternal loss, to the act of dying itself. The more impressionable cadets—Sutton, von Gluck, Ostrander—could not look astern without finding their eyes swimming with tears. Even the suave

Culpepper was awed by the magnificence of the spectacle, the sun an aching pit not to be tolerated, Earth a plump pearl rolling on black velvet among a myriad glittering diamonds. And away from Earth, away from the sun, opened an exalted magnificence of another order entirely. For the first time the cadets became dimly aware that Henry Belt had spoken truly of strange visions. Here was death, here was peace, solitude, star-blazing beauty which promised not oblivion in death, but eternity. . . . Streams and spatters of stars. . . . The familiar constellations, the stars with their prideful names presenting themselves like heroes: Achernar, Fomalhaut, Sadal, Suud, Canopus. . . .

Sutton could not bear to look into the sky. "It's not that I feel fear," he told von Gluck, "or yes, perhaps it is fear. It sucks at me, draws me out there. . . . I suppose in due course I'll become accustomed to it."

"I'm not so sure," said von Gluck. "I wouldn't be surprised if space could become a psychological addition, a need—so that whenever you walked on Earth you felt hot and breathless."

Life settled into a routine. Henry Belt no longer seemed a man, but a capricious aspect of nature, like storm or lightning; and like some natural cataclysm. Henry Belt showed no favoritism, nor forgave one jot or tittle of offense. Apart from the private cubicles, no place on the ship escaped his attention. Always he reeked of whisky, and it became a matter of covert speculation as to exactly how much whisky he had brought aboard. But no matter how he reeked or how he swayed on his feet, his eyes remained clever and steady, and he spoke without slurring in his paradoxically clear, sweet voice.

One day he seemed slightly drunker than usual, and ordered all hands into space suits and out to inspect the sail for meteoric puncture. The order seemed sufficiently odd that the cadets stared at him in disbelief. "Gentlemen, you hesitate, you fail to exert yourselves, you luxuriate in sloth. Do you fancy yourselves at the Riviera? Into the space suits, on the double, and everybody into space. Check hoop, sail, reflector, struts, and sensor. You will be adrift for two hours. When you return I want a comprehensive report. Mr. Lynch, I believe you are in charge of this watch. You will present the report."

"Yes, sir."

"One more matter. You will notice that the sail is slightly bellied by the continual radiation pressure. It therefore acts as a focusing device, the focal point presumably occurring behind the cab. But this is not a matter to be taken for granted. I have seen a man burnt to death in such a freak accident. Bear this in mind."

For two hours the cadets drifted through space, propelled by tanks of gas and thrust tubes. All enjoyed the experience except Sutton, who found himself appalled by the immensity of his emotions. Probably least affected was the practical Verona, who inspected the sail with a care exacting enough even to satisfy Henry Belt.

The next day the computer went wrong. Ostrander was in charge of the watch and knocked on Henry Belt's door to make the report.

Henry Belt appeared in the doorway. He apparently had been asleep. "What is the difficulty, Mr. Ostrander?"

"We're in trouble, sir. The computer has gone out."

Henry Belt rubbed his grizzled pate. "This is not an unusual circumstance. We prepare for this contingency by schooling all cadets thoroughly in computer design and repair. Have you identified the difficulty?"

"The bearings which suspend the data separation disks have broken. The shaft has several millimeters' play and as a result there is total confusion in the data presented to the analyzer."

"An interesting problem. Why do you present it to me?"

"I thought you should be notified, sir. I don't believe we carry spares for this particular bearing."

Henry Belt shook his head sadly. "Mr. Ostrander, do you recall my statement at the beginning of this voyage, that you six gentlemen are totally responsible for the navigation of the ship?"

"Yes, sir. But—"

"This is an applicable situation. You must either repair the computer or perform the calculations yourself."

"Very well, sir. I will do my best."

24

Chapter 5

★ ★ ★

Lynch, Verona, Ostrander, and Sutton disassembled the mechanism, removed the worn bearing. "Confounded antique!" said Lynch. "Why can't they give us descent equipment? Or if they want to kill us, why not shoot us and save us all trouble."

"We're not dead yet," said Verona. "You've looked for a spare?"

"Naturally. There's nothing remotely like this."

Verona looked at the bearing dubiously. "I suppose we could cast a babbitt sleeve and machine it to fit. That's what we'll have to do—unless you fellows are awfully fast with your math."

Sutton glanced out the port, quickly turned away his eyes. "I wonder if we should cut sail."

"Why?" asked Ostrander.

"We don't want to build up too much velocity. We're already going 30 miles a second."

"Mars is a long way off."

"And if we miss, we go shooting past. Then where are we?"

"Sutton, you're a pessimist. A shame to find morbid tendencies in one so young." This from von Gluck.

"I'd rather be a live pessimist than a dead comedian."

The new sleeve was duly cast, machined and fitted. Anxiously the alignment of the data disks was checked. "Well," said Verona dubiously, "there's wobble. How much that affects the functioning remains to be seen. We can take some of it out by shimming the mount. . . ."

Shims of tissue paper were inserted and the wobble

seemed to be reduced. "Now—feed in the data," said Sutton. "Let's see how we stand."

Coordinates were fed into the system; the indicator swung. "Enlarge sail cant four degrees," said von Gluck, "we're making too much left concentric. Projected course . . ." he tapped buttons, watched the bright line extend across the screen, swing around a dot representing the center of gravity of Mars. "I make it an elliptical pass, about twenty thousand miles out. That's at present acceleration, and it should toss us right back at Earth."

"Great. Simply great. Let's go, 25!" This was Lynch. "I've heard of guys dropping flat on their faces and kissing Earth when they put down. Me, I'm going to live in a cave the rest of my life."

Sutton went to look at the data disks. The wobble was slight but perceptible. "Good Lord," he said huskily. "The other end of the shaft is loose too."

Lynch started to spit curses; Verona's shoulders slumped. "Let's get to work and fix it."

Another bearing was cast, machined, polished, mounted. The disks wobbled, scraped. Mars, an ocher disk, shouldered ever closer in from the side. With the computer unreliable, the cadets calculated and plotted the course manually. The results were at slight but significant variance with those of the computer. The cadets looked dourly at each other. "Well," growled Ostrander, "There's error. Is it the instruments? The calculation? The plotting? Or the computer?"

Culpepper said in a subdued voice, "Well, we're not about to crash head-on at any rate."

Verona went back to study the computer. "I can't imagine why the bearings don't work better. . . . The mounting brackets—could they have shifted?" He removed the side housing, studied the frame, then went to the case for tools.

"What are you going to do?" demanded Sutton.

"Try to ease the mounting brackets around. I think that's our trouble."

"Leave me alone! You'll bugger the machine so it'll never work."

26

Verona paused, looked questioningly around the group. "Well? What's the verdict?"

"Maybe we'd better check with the old man," said Ostrander nervously.

"All well and good—but you know what he'll say."

"Let's deal cards. Ace of spades goes to ask him."

Culpepper received the ace. He knocked on Henry Belt's door. There was no response. He started to knock again, but restrained himself.

He returned to the group. "Wait till he shows himself. I'd rather crash into Mars than bring forth Henry Belt and his red book."

The ship crossed the orbit of Mars well ahead of the looming red planet. It came toppling at them with a peculiar clumsy grandeur, a mass obviously bulky and globular, but so fine and clear was the detail, so absent the perspective, that the distance and size might have been anything. Instead of swinging in a sharp elliptical curve back toward Earth, the ship swerved aside in a blunt hyperbola and proceeded outward, now at a velocity of close to fifty miles a second. Mars receded astern and to the side. A new part of space lay ahead. The sun was noticeably smaller. Earth could no longer be differentiated from the stars. Mars departed quickly and politely, and space seemed lonely and forlorn.

Henry Belt had not appeared for two days. At last Culpepper went to knock on the door—once, twice, three times: a strange face looked out. It was Henry Belt, face haggard, skin like pulled taffy. His eyes were red and glared, his hair seemed matted and more unkempt than hair a quarter-inch long should be.

But he spoke in his quiet, clear voice. "Mr. Culpepper, your merciless din has disturbed me. I am quite put out with you."

"Sorry, sir. We feared that you were ill."

Henry Belt made no response. He looked past Culpepper, around the circle of faces. "You gentlemen are unwontedly serious. Has this presumptive illness of mine caused you all distress?"

Sutton spoke in a rush, "The computer is out of order."

"Why then, you must repair it."

"It's a matter of altering the housing. If we do it incorrectly—"

"Mr. Sutton, please do not harass me with the hour-by-hour minutiae of running the ship."

"But, sir, the matter has become serious; we need your advice. We missed the Mars turnaround—"

"Well, I suppose there's always Jupiter. Must I explain the basic elements of astrogation to you?"

"But the computer's out of order—definitely."

"Then, if you wish to return to Earth, you must perform the calculations with pencil and paper. Why is it necessary to explain the obvious?"

"Jupiter is a long way out," said Sutton in a shrill voice. "Why can't we just turn around and go home?" This last was almost a whisper.

"I see I've been too easy on you cads," said Henry Belt. "You stand around idly; you chatter nonsense while the machinery goes to pieces and the ship flies at random. Everybody into space suits for sail inspection. Come now. Let's have some snap. What are you all? Walking corpses? You, Mr. Culpepper, why the delay?"

"It occurred to me, sir, that we are approaching the asteroid belt. As I am chief of the watch I consider it my duty to cant sail to swing us around the area."

"You may do this; then join the rest in hull-and-sail inspection."

"Yes, sir."

The cadets donned space suits, Sutton with the utmost reluctance. Out into the dark void they went, and now here was loneliness indeed.

When they returned, Henry Belt had returned to his compartment.

"As Mr. Belt points out, we have no great choice," said Ostrander. "We missed Mars, so let's hit Jupiter. Luckily it's in good position—otherwise we'd have to swing out to Saturn or Uranus—"

"They're off behind the sun," said Lynch. "Jupiter's out last chance."

"Let's do it right then. I say, let's make one last attempt to set those confounded bearings. . . ."

But now it seemed as if the wobble and twist had been eliminated. The disks tracked perfectly, the accuracy monitor glowed green.

"Great!" yelled Lynch. "Feed it the dope. Let's get going! All sail for Jupiter. Good Lord, but we're having a trip!"

"Wait till it's over," said Sutton. Since his return from sail inspection, he had stood to one side, cheeks pinched, eyes staring. "It's not over yet. And maybe it's not meant to be."

The other five pretended not to have heard him. The computer spat out figures and angles. There were a billion miles to travel. Acceleration was less, due to the diminution in the intensity of sunlight. At least a month must pass before Jupiter came close.

Chapter 6

★ ★ ★

The ship, great sail spread to the fading sunlight, fled like a ghost—out, always out. Each of the cadets had quietly performed the same calculation, and arrived at the same result. If the swing around Jupiter was not performed with exactitude, if the ship was not slung back like a stone on a string, there was nothing beyond. Saturn, Uranus, Neptune, Pluto were far around the sun; the ship, speeding at a hundred miles a second, could not be halted by the waning gravity of the sun, nor yet sufficiently accelerated in a concentric direction by sail and jet into a true orbit. The very nature of the sail made it useless as a brake, always the thrust was outward.

Within the hull seven men lived and thought, and the interrelationships worked and stirred like yeast in a vat of decaying fruit. The fundamental similarity, the human identity of the seven men, was utterly canceled; apparent only were the disparities. Each cadet appeared to others only as a walking characteristic, and Henry Belt was an incomprehensible Thing, who appeared from his compartment at unpredictable times, to move quietly here and there with the blind, blank grin of an archaic Attic hero.

Jupiter loomed and bulked. The ship, at last within reach of the Jovian gravity, sidled over to meet it. The cadets gave ever more careful attention to the computer, checking and counter-checking the instructions. Verona was the most assiduous at this, Sutton the most harassed and ineffectual. Lynch growled and cursed and sweat; Ostrander complained in a thin, peevish voice. Von Gluck worked with the calm of pessimistic fatalism; Culpepper seemed unconcerned, almost debonair; his blandness bewildered Ostrander, infuriated Lynch, awoke a malignant hate in Sutton. Verona and von Gluck, on the other hand seemed to derive strength and refreshment from Culpepper's placid acceptance of the situation. Henry Belt said nothing. Occasionally he emerged from his compartment to survey the wardroom and the cadets with the detached interest of a visitor to an asylum.

It was Lynch who made the discovery. He signaled it with an odd growl of sheer dismay, which brought a resonant questioning sound from Sutton. "My God, my God," muttered Lynch.

Verona was at his side. "What's the trouble?"

"Look. This gear. When we replaced the disks we dephased the whole apparatus one notch. This white dot and this other white dot should synchronize. They're one sprocket apart. All the results would check and be consistent because they'd all be off by the same factor."

Verona sprang into action. Off came the housing, off came various components. Gently he lifted the gear, set it back into correct alignment. The other cadets leaned over him as he worked, except Culpepper who was chief of the watch.

Henry Belt appeared. "You gentlemen are certainly

diligent in your navigation," he said. "Perfectionists almost."

"We do our best," greeted Lynch between set teeth. "It's a damn shame sending us out with a machine like this."

The red book appeared. "Mr. Lynch, I mark you down not for your private sentiments, which are of course yours to entertain, but for voicing them and thereby contributing to an unhealthy atmosphere of despairing and hysterical pessimism."

A tide of red crept up from Lynch's neck. He bent over the computer, made no comment. But Sutton suddenly cried out, "What else do you expect from us? We came out here to learn, not to suffer, or to fly on forever!" He gave a ghastly laugh. Henry Belt listened patiently. "Think of it!" cried Sutton. "The seven of us. In this capsule, forever!"

"I am afraid that I must charge you two demerits for your outburst, Mr. Sutton. A good spaceman maintains his dignity at all costs."

Lynch looked up from the computer. "Well, now we've got a corrected reading. Do you know what it says?"

Henry Belt turned him a look of polite inquiry.

"We're going to miss," said Lynch. "We're going to pass by just as we passed Mars. Jupiter is pulling us around and sending us out toward Gemini."

The silence was thick in the room. Henry Belt turned to look at Culpepper, who was standing by the porthole, photographing Jupiter with his personal camera.

"Mr. Culpepper?"

"Yes, sir."

"You seem unconcerned by the prospect which Mr. Sutton has set forth."

"I hope it's not imminent."

"How do you propose to avoid it?"

"I imagine that we will radio for help, sir."

"You forget that I have destroyed the radio."

"I remember noting a crate marked 'Radio Parts' stored in the starboard jet-pod."

"I am sorry to disillusion you, Mr. Culpepper. That case is mislabeled."

Ostrander jumped to his feet, left the wardroom. There was the sound of moving crates. A moment of silence. Then he returned. He glared at Henry Belt. "Whisky. Bottles of whisky."

Henry Belt nodded. "I told you as much."

"But now we have no radio," said Lynch in an ugly voice.

"We never have had a radio, Mr. Lynch. You were warned that you would have to depend on your own resources to bring us home. You have failed, and in the process doomed me as well as yourself. Incidentally, I must mark you all down ten demerits for a faulty cargo check."

"Demerits," said Ostrander in a bleak voice.

"Now, Mr. Culpepper," said Henry Belt. "What is your next proposal?"

"I don't know, sir."

Verona spoke in a placatory voice. "What would you do, sir, if you were in our position?"

Henry Belt shook his head. "I am an imaginative man, Mr. Verona, but there are certain leaps of the mind which are beyond my powers." He returned to his compartment.

Von Gluck looked curiously at Culpepper. "It is a fact. You're not at all concerned."

"Oh, I'm concerned. But I believe that Mr. Belt wants to get home too. He's too good a spaceman not to know exactly what he's doing."

The door from Henry Belt's compartment slid back. Henry Belt stood in the opening. "Mr. Culpepper, I chanced to overhear your remark, and I now note down ten demerits against you. This attitude expresses a complacence as dangerous as Mr. Sutton's utter funk." He looked about the room. "Pay no heed to Mr. Culpepper. He is wrong. Even if I could repair this disaster, I would not raise a hand. For I expect to die in space."

Chapter 7

The sail was canted vectorless, edgewise to the sun. Jupiter was a smudge astern. There were five cadets in the wardroom. Culpepper, Verona, and von Gluck sat talking in low voices. Ostrander and Lynch lay crouched, arms to knees, faces to the wall. Sutton had gone two days before. Quietly donning his space suit, he had stepped into the exit chamber and thrust himself headlong into space. A propulsion unit gave him added speed, and before any of the cadets could intervene he was gone.

Shortly thereafter Lynch and Ostrander succumbed to inanition, a kind of despondent helplessness: manic-depression in its most stupefying phase. Culpepper the suave, Verona the pragmatic, and von Gluck the sensitive remained.

They spoke quietly to themselves, out of earshot of Henry Belt's room. "I still believe," said Culpepper, "that somehow there is a means to get ourselves out of this mess, and that Henry Belt knows it."

Verona said, "I wish I could think so. . . . We've been over it a hundred times. If we set sail for Saturn or Neptune or Uranus, the outward vector of thrust plus the outward vector of our momentum will take us far beyond Pluto before we're anywhere near. The plasma jets could stop us if we had enough energy, but the shield can't supply it, and we don't have another power source. . . ."

Von Gluck hit his fist into his hand. "Gentlemen," he said in a soft delighted voice, "I believe we have sufficient energy at hand. We will use the sail. Remember? It is bellied. It can function as a mirror. It spreads five square miles of surface. Sunlight out here is thin—but so long as we collect enough of it—"

"I understand!" said Culpepper. "We back off the hull till the reactor is at the focus of the sail and turn on the jets!"

Verona said dubiously, "We'll still be receiving radiation pressure. And what's worse, the jets will impinge back on the sail. Effect—cancellation. We'll be nowhere."

"If we cut the center out of the sail—just enough to allow the plasma through—we'd beat that objection. And as for the radiation pressure—we'll surely do better with the plasma drive."

"What do we use to make plasma? We don't have the stock."

"Anything that can be ironized. The radio, the computer, your shoes, my shirt, Culpepper's camera, Henry Belt's whisky. . . ."

Chapter 8

★　★　★

The angel-wagon came up to meet Sail 25, in orbit beside Sail 40, which was just making ready to take out a new crew.

The cargo carrier drifted near, eased into position. Three men sprang across to Sail 40, a few hundred yards behind 25, tossed lines back to the carrier, pulled bales of cargo and equipment across the gap.

The five cadets and Henry Belt, clad in space suits, stepped out into the sunlight. Earth spread below, green and blue, white and brown, the contours so precious and dear as to bring tears to the eyes. The cadets transferring cargo to Sail 40 gazed at them curiously as they worked.

34

At last they were finished, and the six men of Sail 25 boarded the carrier.

"Back safe and sound, eh Henry?" said the pilot. "Well, I'm always surprised."

Henry Belt made no answer. The cadets stowed their cargo, and standing by the port, took a final look at Sail 25. The carrier retro-jetted; the two sails seemed to rise above them.

The lighter nosed in and out of the atmosphere; then braking, it extended its wings and glided to an easy landing on the Mojave Desert.

The cadets, their legs suddenly loose and weak to the unaccustomed gravity, limped after Henry Belt to the carry-all, seated themselves, and were conveyed to the administration complex. They alighted from the carry-all, and now Henry Belt motioned the five to the side.

"Here, gentlemen, is where I leave you. Tonight I will check my red book and prepare my official report. But I believe I can present you an unofficial resumé of my impressions. Mr. Lynch and Mr. Ostrander, I feel that you are ill-suited either for command or for any situation which might inflict prolonged emotional pressure upon you. I cannot recommend you for space duty.

"Mr. von Gluck, Mr. Culpepper, and Mr. Verona, all of you meet my minimum requirements for a recommendation, although I shall write the words 'Especially Recommended' only beside the names 'Clyde von Gluck' and 'Marcus Verona.' You brought the sail back to Earth by essentially faultless navigation.

"So now our association ends. I trust you have profited by it." Henry Belt nodded briefly to each of the five and limped off around the building.

The cadets looked after him. Culpepper reached in his pocket and brought forth a pair of small metal objects which he displayed in his palm. "Recognize these?"

"Hmf," said Lynch in a flat voice. "Bearings for the computer disks. The original ones."

"I found them in the little spare-parts tray. They weren't there before."

Von Gluck nodded. "The machinery always seemed to fail immediately after sail check, as I recall."

"Lynch drew in his breath with a sharp hiss. He turned, strode away. Ostrander followed him. Culpepper shrugged. To Verona he gave one of the bearings, to von Gluck the other. "For souvenirs—or medals. You fellows deserve them."

"Thanks, Ed," said von Gluck.

"Thanks," muttered Verona. "I'll make a stickpin of this thing."

The three, not able to look at each other, glanced up into the sky where the first stars of twilight were appearing, then continued on into the building where family and friends and sweethearts awaited them.

DODKIN'S JOB

The Theory of Organized Society (as developed by Kinch, Kolbig, Penton, and others) yields such a wealth of significant information, revealing manifold intricacies and portentous projections, that occasionally it is well to consider its deceptively simple major premise (here stated by Kolbig):

> When self-willed microunits combine to form and sustain a durable macrounit, certain freedoms of action are curtailed.
>
> This is the basic process of Organization.
>
> The more numerous and erratic the microunits, the more complex must be the structure and function of the macrounit—hence the more pervasive and restricting the details of Organization.

> —from Leslie Penton, *First Principles of Organization*

The general population of the city had become forgetful of curtailed freedoms, as a snake no longer remembers the legs of its forebears. Somewhere someone has stated, "When the discrepancy between the theory and practice of a culture is very great, this indicates that the culture is undergoing rapid change." By such a test the culture of the city was stable, if not static. The population ordered their lives by schedule, classification, and precedent, satisfied with the bland rewards of Organization.

But in the healthiest tissue bacteria exist, and the most negligible impurity flaws a critical crystallization.

Luke Grogatch was forty, thin and angular, dour of forehead, with a sardonic cast to his mouth and eyebrows and a sideways twist to his head as if he suffered from earache. He was too astute to profess Nonconformity; too perverse to strive for improved status; too pessimistic, captious, sarcastic, and outspoken to keep the jobs to which he found himself assigned. Each new reclassification depressed his status; he disliked each new job with increasing fervor.

Finally, rated as *Flunky/Class D/Unskilled*, Luke was dispatched to the District 8892 Sewer Maintenance Department and from there ordered out as night-shift swamper on Tunnel Gang Number 3's rotary drilling machine.

Reporting for work, Luke presented himself to the gang foreman, Fedor Miskitman, a big, buffalo-faced man with flaxen hair and placid blue eyes. Miskitman produced a shovel and took Luke to a position close up behind the drilling machine's cutting head. Here, said Miskitman, was Luke's station. Luke would be required to keep the tunnel floor clean of loose rock and gravel. When the tunnel broke through into an old sewer, there would be scale and that detritus known as "wet waste" to remove. Luke was to keep the dust trap clean and in optimum adjustment. During the breaks he would lubricate those bearings isolated from the automatic lubrication system, and he was to replace broken teeth on the cutting head whenever necessary.

Luke inquired if this was the extent of his duties, his voice strong with an irony the guileless Fedor Miskitman failed to notice.

"That is all," said Miskitman. He handed Luke the shovel. "Mostly it is the trash. The floor must be clean."

Luke suggested to the foreman a modification of the hopper jaws which would tend to eliminate the spill of broken rock; in fact, went Luke's argument, why bother at all? Let the rock lie where it fell. The concrete lining of the tunnel would mask so trivial a scatter of gravel.

Miskitman dismissed the suggestion out of hand: the rock must be removed. When Luke asked why, Miskitman told him, "That is the way the job is done."

Luke made a rude noise under his breath. He tested the shovel and shook his head in dissatisfaction. The handle was too long, the blade too short. He reported this fact to

38

Miskitman, who merely glanced at his watch and signaled to the drill operator. The machine whined into revolution and with an ear-splitting roar made contact with the rock. Miskitman departed, and Luke went back to work.

During the shift he found that if he worked in a half-crouch most of the hot, dust-laden exhaust from the machine would pass over his head. Changing a cutting tooth during the first rest period he burned a blister on his left thumb. At the end of the shift a single consideration deterred Luke from declaring himself unqualified: he would be declassified from *Flunky/Class D/Unskilled* to *Junior Executive,* with a corresponding cut in expense account. Such a declassification would take him to the very bottom of the Status List, and so could not be countenanced; his present expense account was barely adequate, covering nutrition at a Type RP Victualing Service, sleeping space in a Sublevel 22 dormitory, and sixteen Special Coupons per month. He took Class 14 Erotic Processing, and was allowed twelve hours per month at his recreation club, with optional use of barbells, table-tennis equipment, two miniature bowling alleys, and any of the six telescreens tuned permanently to Band H. Luke often daydreamed of a more sumptuous life: AAA nutrition, a suite of rooms for his exclusive use, Special Coupons by the bale, Class 7 Erotic Processing, or even Class 6, or 5: despite Luke's contempt for the High Echelon he had no quarrel with High Echelon perquisites. And always as a bitter coda to the daydreams came the conviction that he might have been enjoying these good things in all reality. He had watched his fellows jockeying; he knew all the tricks and techniques: the beavering, the gregariousness, the smutting, knuckling. . . . Why not make use of this knowledge?

"I'd rather be Class D Flunky," sneered Luke to himself.

Occasionally a measure of doubt would seep into Luke's mind. Perhaps he merely lacked the courage to compete, to come to grips with the world! And the seep of doubt would become a trickle of self-contempt. A Nonconformist, that's what he was—and he lacked the courage to admit it!

39

Then Luke's obstinacy would reassert itself. Why admit to Nonconformity when it meant a trip to the Disorganized House? A fool's trick—and Luke was no fool. Perhaps he was a Nonconformist in all reality; again, perhaps not—he had never really made up his mind. He presumed that he was suspected; occasionally he intercepted queer side glances and significant jerks of the head among his fellow workers. Let them leer. They could prove nothing.

But now . . . he was Luke Grogatch, Class D Flunky, separated by a single status from the nonclassified sediment of criminals, idiots, children, and proved Nonconformists. Luke Grogatch, who had dreamed such dreams of the High Echelon, of pride and independence! Instead —Luke Grogatch, Class D Flunky. Taking orders from a hay-headed lunk, working with semiskilled laborers with status almost as low as his own: Luke Grogatch, flunky.

Seven weeks passed. Luke's dislike for his job became a mordant passion. The work was arduous, hot, repellent. Fedor Miskitman turned an uncomprehending gaze on Luke's most rancorous grimaces, grunted and shrugged at Luke's suggestions and arguments. This was the way things were done—his manner implied—always had been done, and always would be done.

Fedor Miskitman received a daily policy directive from the works superintendent which he read to the crew during the first rest break of the shift. These directives generally dealt with such matters as work norms, team spirit, and cooperation; pleas for a finer polish on the concrete; warnings against off-shift indulgence which might dull enthusiasm and decrease work efficiency. Luke usually paid small heed, until one day Fedor Miskitman, pulling out the familiar yellow sheet, read in his stolid voice:

PUBLIC WORKS DEPARTMENT, PUBLIC UTILITIES DIVISION
AGENCY OF SANITARY WORKS, DISTRICT 8892
SEWAGE DISPOSAL SECTION

Bureau of Sewer Construction and Maintenance
Office of Procurement

Policy Directive: 6511 Series BV96
Order Code: GZP—AAR—REG

Reference:	G98—7542
Date Code:	BT—EQ—LLT
Authorized:	LL8—P—SC 8892
Checked:	48
Counterchecked:	92C

From: Lavester Limon, Manager, Office of Procurement

Through: All construction and maintenance offices

To: All construction and maintenance superinten-
dents

Attention: All job foremen

Subject: Tool longevity, the promotion
thereof

Instant of Application: Immediate

Duration of Relevance: Permanent

Substance: At beginning of each shift all hand tools
shall be checked out of District 8892 Sewer
Maintenance Warehouse. At close of each
shift all hand tools shall be carefully
cleaned and returned to District 8892
Sewer Maintenance Warehouse.

Directive reviewed and transmitted: Butry Keghorn, General Superintendent
of Construction, Bu-
reau of Sewer Con-
struction

Clyde Kaddo, Super-
intendent of Sewer
Maintenance

As Fedor Miskitman read the "Substance" section,
Luke expelled his breath in an incredulous snort. Miskitman finished, folded the sheet with careful movements of
his thick fingers, looked at his watch. "That is the directive. We are twenty-five seconds over time; we must get
back to work."

"Just a minute," said Luke. "One or two things about
that directive I want explained."

Miskitman turned his mild gaze upon Luke. "You did
not understand it?"

"Not altogether. Who does it apply to?"

"It is an order for the entire gang."

41

"What do they mean, 'hand tools'?"

"These are tools which are held in the hands."

"Does that mean a shovel?"

"A shovel?" Miskitman shrugged his burly shoulders. "A shovel is a hand tool."

Luke asked in a voice of hushed wonder: "They want me to polish my shovel, carry it four miles to the warehouse, then pick it up tomorrow and carry it back here?"

Miskitman unfolded the directive, held it at arm's length, and read with moving lips. "That is the order." He refolded the paper and returned it to his pocket.

Luke again feigned astonishment. "Certainly there's a mistake."

"A mistake?" Miskitman was puzzled. "Why should there be a mistake?"

"They can't be serious," said Luke. "It's not only ridiculous, it's peculiar."

"I do not know," said Miskitman incuriously. "To work. We are late one minute and a half."

"I assume that all this cleaning and transportation is done on Organization time," Luke suggested.

Miskitman unfolded the directive, held it at arm's length, read. "It does not say so. Our quota is not different." He folded the directive and put it in his pocket.

Luke spat on the rock floor. "I'll bring my own shovel. Let 'em carry around their own precious hand tools."

Miskitman scratched his chin and once more reread the directive. He shook his head dubiously. "The order says that all hand tools must be cleaned and taken to the warehouse. It does not say who owns the tools."

Luke could hardly speak for exasperation. "You know what I think of that directive?"

Fedor Miskitman paid him no heed. "To work. We are overtime."

"If I were general superintendent—" Luke began, but Miskitman rumbled roughly.

"We do not earn perquisites by talking. To work. We are late."

The rotary cutter started up; seventy-two teeth snarled into gray-brown sandstone. Hopper jaws swallowed the chunks, passing them down an epiglottis into a feeder gut which evacuated far down the tunnel into life-buckets. Stray chips rained upon the tunnel floor, which Luke Grogatch must scrape up and return into the hopper. Behind Luke two reinforcement men flung steel hoops into place, flash-welding them to longitudinal bars with quick pinches of the fingers, contact-plates in their gauntlets discharging the requisite gout of energy. Behind came the concrete-spray man, mix hissing out of his revolving spider, followed by two finishers, nervous men working with furious energy, stroking the concrete into a glossy polish. Fedor Miskitman marched back and forth, testing the reinforcement, gauging the thickness of the concrete, making frequent progress checks on the chart to the rear of the rotary cutter, where an electronic device traced the course of the tunnel, guiding it through the system of conduits, ducts, passages, pipes, and tubes for water, air, gas, steam, transportation, freight, and communication which knit the city into an organized unit.

The night shift ended at four o'clock in the morning. Miskitman made careful entries in his log; the concrete-spray man blew out his nozzles; the reinforcement workers removed their gauntlets, power packs, and insulating garments. Luke Grogatch straightened, rubbed his sore back, and stood glowering at the shovel. He felt Miskitman's ox-calm scrutiny. If he threw the shovel to the side of the tunnel as usual and marched off about his business, he would be guilty of disorganized conduct. The penalty, as Luke knew well, was declassification. Luke stared at the shovel, fuming with humiliation. Conform or be declassified. Submit—or become a Junior Executive.

Luke heaved a deep sigh. The shovel was clean enough; one or two swipes with a rag would remove the dust. But there was the ride by crowded man-belt to the warehouse, the queue at the window, the check-in, the added distance to his dormitory. Tomorrow the process must be repeated. Why the necessity for this added effort? Luke knew well enough. An obscure functionary somewhere along the chain of bureaus and commissions had been at a loss for a means to display his diligence. What better method than concern for valuable city property?

Consequently the absurd directive, filtering down to Fedor Miskitman and ultimately to Luke Grogatch, the victim. What joy to meet this osbscure functionary face to face, to tweak his sniveling nose, to kick his craven rump along the corridors of his own office. . . .

Fedor Miskitman's voice disturbed his reverie. "Clean your shovel. It is the end of the shift."

Luke made token resistance. "The shovel is clean," he growled. "This is the most absurd antic I've ever been co-erced into. If only I—"

Fedor Miskitman, in a voice as calm and unhurried as a deep river, said, "If you do not like the policy, you should put a petition in the suggestion box. That is the privilege of all. Until the policy is changed you must con-form. That is the way we live. That is Organization, and we are Organized men."

"Let me see that directive," Luke barked. "I'll get it changed. I'll cram it down somebody's throat. I'll—"

"You must wait until it is logged. Then you may have it; it is useless to me."

"I'll wait," said Luke between clenched teeth.

With method and deliberation Fedor Miskitman made a final check of the job, inspecting machinery, the teeth of the cutter head, the nozzles of the spider, the discharge belt. He went to his little desk at the rear of the rotary drill, noted progress, signed expense-account vouchers, fi-nally registered the policy directive on minifilm. Then with a ponderous sweep of his arm he tendered the yellow sheet to Luke. "What will you do with it?"

"I'll find who formed this idiotic policy. I'll tell him what I think of it and what I think of him, to boot."

Miskitman shook his head in disapproval. "That is not the way such things should be done."

"How would you do it?" asked Luke with a wolfish grin.

Miskitman considered, pursing his lips, jerking his bris-tling eyebrows. At last with great simplicity of manner he said, "I would not do it."

Luke threw up his hands and set off down the tunnel. Miskitman's voice boomed against his back. "You must take the shovel!"

Luke halted. Slowly he faced about, glared back at the hulking figure of the foreman. Obey the policy directive or be declassified. With slow steps, with hanging head and averted eyes, he retraced his path. Snatching the shovel, he stalked back down the tunnel. His bony shoulder blades were exposed and sensitive; Fedor Miskitman's mild blue gaze, following him, seemed to scrape the nerves of his back.

Ahead the tunnel extended, a glossy pale sinus, dwindling back along the distance they had bored. Through some odd trick of refraction alternate bright and dark rings circled the tube, confusing the eye, creating a hypnotic semblance of two-dimensionality. Luke shuffled drearily into this illusory bull's-eye, dazed with shame and helplessness, the shovel a load of despair. Had he come to this—Luke Grogatch, previously so arrogant in his cynicism and barely concealed Nonconformity? Must he cringe at last, submit slavishly to witless regulations? . . . If only he were a few places further up the list! Drearily he pictured the fine incredulous shock with which he would have greeted the policy directive, the sardonic nonchalance with which he would have let the shovel fall from his limp hands. . . . Too late, too late! Now he must toe the mark, must carry his shovel dutifully to the warehouse. In a spasm of rage he flung the blameless implement clattering down the tunnel ahead of him. Nothing he could do! Nowhere to turn! No way to strike back! Organization: smooth and relentless; Organization: massive and inert, tolerant of the submissive, serenely cruel to the unbeliever . . . Luke came to his shovel and, whispering an obscenity, snatched it up and half-ran down the pallid tunnel.

He climbed through a manhole and emerged upon the deck of the 1123rd Avenue Hub, where he was instantly absorbed in the crowds trampling between the man-belts, which radiated like spokes, and the various escalators. Clasping the shovel to his chest, Luke struggled aboard the Fontego man-belt and rushed south, in a direction opposite to that of his dormitory. He rode ten minutes to Astoria Hub, dropped a dozen levels of the Grimesby College Escalator, and crossed a gloomy dank area smelling of old rock to a local feeder-belt which carried him to the District 8892 Sewer Maintenance Warehouse.

Luke found the warehouse brightly lit, the center of considerable activity, with several hundred men coming and going. Those coming, like Luke, carried tools; those going went empty-handed.

Luke joined the line which had formed in front of the tool storeroom. Fifty or sixty men preceded him, a drab centipede of arms, shoulders, heads, legs, the tools projecting to either side. The centipede moved slowly, the men exchanging badinage and quips.

Observing their patience, Luke's normal irascibility asserted itself. Look at them, he thought, standing like sheep, jumping to attention at the rustle of an unfolding directive. Did they inquire about the reason for the order? Did they question the necessity for their inconvenience? No! The louts stood chuckling and chatting, accepting the directive as one of life's incalculable vicissitudes, something elemental and arbitrary, like the changing of the seasons. . . . And he, Luke Grogatch, was he better or worse? The question burned in Luke's throat like the aftertaste of vomit.

Still, better or worse, where was his choice? Conform or declassify. A poor choice. There was always the recourse of the suggestion box, as Fedor Miskitman, perhaps in bland jest, had pointed out. Luke growled in disgust. Weeks later he might receive a printed form with one statement of a multiple-choice list checked off by some clerical flunky or junior executive: "The situation described by your petition is already under study by responsible officials. Thank you for your interest." Or, "The situation described by your petition is temporary and may shortly be altered. Thank you for your interest." Or, "The situation described by your petition is the product of established policy and is not subject to change. Thank you for your interest."

A novel thought occurred to Luke; he might exert himself and reclassify *up* the list. . . . As soon as the idea arrived he dismissed it. In the first place he was close to middle age; too many young men were pushing up past him. Even if he could goad himself into the competition . . .

The line moved slowly forward. Behind Luke a plump little man sagged under the weight of a Velstro inchskip. A forelock of light brown floss dangled over his moony face; his mouth was puckered into a rosebud of concentration; his eyes were absurdly serious. He wore a rather dapper pink and brown coverall with orange ankle-boots and a blue beret with the three orange pompoms affected by the Velstro technicians.

Between shabby, sour-mouthed Luke and this short moony man in the dandy's overalls existed so basic a difference that an immediate mutual dislike was inevitable.

The short man's prominent hazel eyes rested on Luke's shovel, traveled thoughtfully over Luke's dirt-stained trousers and jacket. He turned his eyes to the side.

"Come a long way?" Luke asked maliciously.

"Not far," said the moon-faced man.

"Worked overtime, eh?" Luke winked. "A bit of quiet beavering, nothing like it—or so I'm told."

"We finished the job," said the plump man, with dignity. "Beavering doesn't enter into it. Why spend half tomorrow's shift on five minutes' work we could do tonight?"

"I know a reason," said Luke wisely. "To do your fellow man a good one in the eye."

The moon-faced man twisted his mouth in a quick uncertain smile, then decided that the remark was not humorous. "That's not my way of working," he said stiffly.

"That thing must be heavy," said Luke, noting how the plump little arms struggled and readjusted to the irregular contours of the tool.

"Yes," came the reply. "It is heavy."

"An hour and a half," intoned Luke. "That's how long it's taking me to park this shovel. Just because somebody up the list has a nightmare. And we poor hoodlums at the bottom suffer."

"I'm not at the bottom of the list. I'm a Technical Tool Operator."

"No difference," said Luke. "The hour and a half is the same. Just for somebody's silly notion."

47

"It's not really so silly," said the moon-faced man. "I fancy there is a good reason for the policy."

Luke shook the shovel by its handle. "And so I have to carry this back and forth along the man-belt three hours a day?"

The little man pursed his lips. "The author of the directive undoubtedly knows his business very well. Otherwise he'd not hold his classification."

"Just who is this unsung hero?" sneered Luke. "I'd like to meet him. I'd like to learn why he wants me to waste three hours a day."

The short man now regarded Luke as he might an insect in his victual ration. "You talk like a Nonconformist. Excuse me if I seem offensive."

"Why apologize for something you can't help?" asked Luke and turned his back.

He flung his shovel to the clerk behind the wicket and received a check. Elaborately Luke turned to the moon-faced man and tucked the check into the breast pocket of the pink and brown coveralls. "You keep this; you'll be using that shovel before I will."

He stalked proudly out of the warehouse. A grand gesture, but—he hesitated before stepping on the man-belt—was it sensible? The technical tool operator in the pink and brown coveralls came out of the warehouse behind him, giving him a queer glance, and hurried away.

Luke looked back into the warehouse. If he returned now he could set things right, and tomorrow there'd be no trouble. If he stormed off to his dormitory, it meant another declassification. Luke Grogatch, Junior Executive. Luke reached into his jumper and took out the policy directive he had acquired from Fedor Miskitman: a bit of yellow paper, printed with a few lines of type, a trivial thing in itself—but it symbolized the Organization: massive force in irresistible operation. Nervously Luke plucked at the paper and looked back into the warehouse. The tool operator had called him a Nonconformist; Luke's mouth squirmed in a brief, weary grimace. It wasn't true. Luke was not a Nonconformist; Luke was nothing in particular. And he needed his bed, his nutrition ticket, his meager expense account. Luke groaned quietly—almost a whisper. The end of the road. He had gone as far as he could go; had he ever thought he could defeat the Organization? Maybe he was wrong and everyone else was right. Possible, thought Luke without conviction. Miskitman seemed content enough; the technical tool operator seemed not only content but complacent. Luke leaned against the warehouse wall, eyes burning and moist with self-pity. Nonconformist. Misfit. What was he going to do?

He curled his lip spitefully, stepped forward onto the man-belt. Devil take them all! They could declassify him; he'd become a junior executive and laugh!

In subdued spirits Luke rode back to the Grimesby Hub. Here, about to board the escalator, he stopped short, blinking and rubbing his long sallow chin, considering still another aspect to the matter. It seemed to offer the chance of—but no. Hardly likely . . . and yet, why not? Once again he examined the directive. Lavester Limon, Manager of the District Office of Procurement, presumably had issued the policy; Lavester Limon could rescind it. If Luke could so persuade Limon, his troubles, while not dissipated, at least would be lessened. He could report shovel-less to his job; he could return sardonic grin for bland hidden grin with Fedor Miskitman. He might even go to the trouble of locating the moon-faced little technical tool operator with the inchskip. . . .

Luke sighed. Why continue this futile daydream? First Lavester Limon must be induced to rescind the directive—and what were the odds of this? . . . Perhaps not astronomical, after all, mused Luke as he rode the man-belt back to his dormitory. The directive clearly was impractical. It worked an inconvenience on many people, while accomplishing very little. If Lavester Limon could be persuaded of this, if he could be shown that his own prestige and reputation were suffering, he might agree to recall the ridiculous directive.

Luke arrived at his dormitory shortly after seven. He went immediately to the communication booth, called the District 8892 Office of Procurement. Lavester Limon, he was told, would be arriving at eight-thirty.

Luke made a careful toilet, and after due consideration

invested four Special Coupons in a fresh set of fibers: a tight black jacket and blue trousers of somewhat martial cut, of considerably better quality than his usual costume. Surveying himself in the washroom mirror, Luke felt that he cut not so poor a figure.

He took his morning quota of nutrition at a nearby Type RP Victualing Service, then ascended to the Sublevel 14 and rode the man-belt to District 8892 Bureau of Sewer Construction and Maintenance.

A pert office girl, dark hair pulled forward over her face in the modish "robber baron" style, conducted Luke into Lavester Limon's office. At the door she glanced demurely backward, and Luke was glad that he had invested in new clothes. Responding to the stimulus, he threw back his shoulders and marched confidently into Lavester Limon's office.

Lavester Limon, sitting at his desk, bumped briefly to his feet in courteous acknowledgment—an amiable-seeming man of middle stature, golden-brown hair brushed carefully across a freckled and suntanned bald spot; golden-brown eyes, round and easy; a golden-brown lounge jacket and trousers of fine golden-brown corduroy. He waved his arm at a chair. "Won't you sit down, Mr. Grogatch?"

In the presence of so much cordiality Luke relaxed his truculence, and even felt a burgeoning of hope. Limon seemed a decent sort; perhaps the directive was, after all, an administrative error.

Limon raised his golden-brown eyebrows inquiringly.

Luke wasted no time on preliminaries. He brought forth the directive. "My business concerns this, Mr. Limon: a policy which you seem to have formulated."

Limon took the directive, read, nodded. "Yes, that's my policy. Something wrong?"

Luke felt surprise and a pang of premonition: surely so reasonable a man must instantly perceive the folly of the directive!

"It's simply not a workable policy," said Luke earnestly. "In fact, Mr. Limon, it's completely unreasonable!"

Lavester Limon seemed not at all offended. "Well, well! And why do you say that? Incidentally, Mr. Grogatch, you're . . ." Again the golden-brown eyebrows arched inquiringly.

"I'm a flunky, Class D, on a tunnel gang," said Luke. "Today it took me an hour and a half to check my shovel. Tomorrow, there'll be another hour and a half checking the shovel out. All on my own time. I don't think that's reasonable."

Lavester Limon reread the directive, pursed his lips, nodded his head once or twice. He spoke into his desk phone. "Miss Rab, I'd like to see—" he consulted the directive's reference number—"Item seven-five-four-two, File G ninety-eight." To Luke he said in rather an absent voice: "Sometimes these things become a trifle complicated."

"But can you change the policy?" Luke burst out. "Do you agree that it's unreasonable?"

Limon cocked his head to the side, made a doubtful grimace. "We'll see what's on the reference. If my memory serves me . . ." His voice faded away.

Twenty seconds passed. Limon tapped his fingers on his desk. A soft chime sounded. Limon touched a button and his desk-screen exhibited the item he had requested: another policy directive similar in form to the first.

PUBLIC WORKS DEPARTMENT, PUBLIC UTILITIES DIVISION
AGENCY OF SANITARY WORKS, DISTRICT 8892
SEWAGE DISPOSAL SECTION

Director's Office

Policy Directive:	2888 Series BQ008
Order Code:	GZP—AAR—REF
Reference:	OP9 123
Date Code:	BR—EQ—LLT
Authorized:	JR D-SDS
Checked:	AC
Counterchecked:	CX McD

From: Judiath Ripp, Director
Through:
To: Lavester Limon, Manager, Office of Procurement
Attention:

Subject:	Economies of operation
Instant of Application:	Immediate
Duration of Relevance:	Permanent

Substance: Your monthly quota of supplies for disbursement Type A, B, D, F, H is hereby reduced 2.2%. It is suggested that you advise affected personnel of this reduction, and take steps to insure most stringent economies. It has been noticed that department use of supplies Type D in particular is in excess of calculated norm.

Suggestion: Greater care by individual users of tools, including warehouse storage at night.

Type D supplies," said Lavester Limon wryly, "are hand tools. Old Ripp wants stringent economies. I merely pass along the word. That's the story behind six-five-one-one." He returned the directive in question to Luke and leaned back in his seat. "I can see how you're exercised, but—" he raised his hands in a careless, almost flippant gesture—"that's the way the Organization works."

Luke sat rigid with disappointment. "Then you won't revoke the directive?"

"My dear fellow! How can I?"

Luke made an attempt at reckless nonchalance. "Well, there's always room for me among the junior executives. I told them where to put their shovel."

"Mmmf. Rash. Sorry I can't help." Limon surveyed Luke curiously, and his lips curved in a faint grin. "Why don't you tackle old Ripp?"

Luke squinted sideways in suspicion. "What good will that do?"

"You never know," said Limon breezily. "Suppose lightning strikes—suppose he rescinds his directive? I can't agitate with him myself; I'd get in trouble—but there's no reason why you can't." He turned Luke a quick, knowing smile, and Luke understood that Lavester Limon's amiability, while genuine, served as a useful camouflage for self-interest and artful playing of the angles.

Luke rose abruptly to his feet. He played cat's-paw for no one, and he opened his mouth to tell Lavester Limon as much. In that instant a recollection crossed his mind: the scene in the warehouse, where he had contemptuously tossed the check for his shovel to the technical tool operator. Always Luke had been prone to the grand gesture, the reckless commitment which left him no scope for retreat. When would he learn self-control? In a subdued voice Luke asked, "Who is this Ripp again?"

"Judiath Ripp, Director of the Sewage Disposal Section. You may have difficulty getting in to see him; he's a troublesome old brute. Wait, I'll find out if he's at his office."

He made inquiries into his desk phone. Information returned to the effect that Judiath Ripp had just arrived at the Section office on Sublevel 3, under Bramblebury Park.

Limon gave Luke tactical advice. "He's choleric—something of a barker. Here's the secret: pay no attention to him. He respects firmness. Pound the table. Roar back at him. If you pussyfoot he'll sling you out. Give him tit for tat and he'll listen."

Luke looked hard at Lavester Limon, well aware that the twinkle in the golden-brown eyes was malicious glee. He said, "I'd like a copy of that directive, so he'll know what I'm talking about."

Limon sobered instantly. Luke could read his mind: *Will Ripp hold it against me if I send up this crackpot? It's worth the chance.* "Sure," said Limon. "Pick it up from the girl."

Luke ascended to Sublevel 3 and walked through the pleasant trilevel arcade below Bramblebury Park. He passed the tall, glass-walled fishtank open to the sky and illuminated by sunlight, boarded the local man-belt, and after a ride of two or three minutes alighted in front of the District 8892 Agency of Sanitary Works.

The Sewage Disposal Section occupied a rather pretentious suite off a small courtyard garden. Luke walked along a passage tiled with blue, gray, and green mosaic and entered a white room furnished in pale gray and pink. A long mural of cleverly twisted gold, black, and white tubing decorated one wall; another was swathed in heavy green leaves growing from a chest-high planter. At a desk sat the receptionist, a plump pouty blonde girl with a simulated bone through her nose and a shark's-tooth

53

necklace dangling around her neck. She wore her hair tied up over her head like a sheaf of wheat, and an amusing black and brown primitive symbol decorated her forehead.

Luke explained that he wished a few words with Mr. Judiath Ripp, Director of the Section.

Perhaps from uneasiness, Luke spoke brusquely. The girl, blinking in surprise, examined him curiously. After a moment's hesitation she shook her head doubtfully. "Won't someone else do? Mr. Ripp's day is tightly scheduled. What did you want to see him about?"

Luke, attempting a persuasive smile, achieved instead a leer of sinister significance. The girl was frankly startled.

"Perhaps you'll tell Mr. Ripp I'm here," said Luke. "One of his policy directives—well, there have been irregularities, or rather a misapplication—"

"Irregularities?" The girl seemed to hear only the single word. She gazed at Luke with new eyes, observing the crisp new black and blue garments with their quasi-military cut. Some sort of inspector? "I'll call Mr. Ripp," she said nervously. "Your name, sir, and status?"

"Luke Grogatch. My status—" Luke smiled once more, and the girl averted her eyes. "It's not important."

"I'll call Mr. Ripp, sir. One moment, if you please." She swung around, murmured anxiously into her screen, looked at Luke, and spoke again. A thin voice rasped a reply. The girl swung back around and nodded at Luke. "Mr. Ripp can spare a few minutes. The first door, please."

Luke walked with stiff shoulders into a tall, wood-paneled room, one wall of which displayed green-glowing tanks of darting red and yellow fish. At the desk sat Judiath Ripp, a tall, heavy man, himself resembling a large fish. His head was narrow, pale as mackerel, and rested backward-tilting on his shoulders. He had no perceptible chin; the neck ran up to his carplike mouth. Pale eyes stared at Luke over small round nostrils; a low brush of hair thrust up from the rear of his head like dry grass over a sand dune. Luke remembered Lavester Limon's verbal depiction of Ripp: "choleric." Hardly appropriate. Had Limon a grudge against Ripp? Was he using Luke as

54

an instrument of mischievous revenge? Suspecting as much, Luke felt uncomfortable and awkward.

Judiath Ripp surveyed him with cold unblinking eyes. "What can I do for you, Mr. Grogatch? My secretary tells me you are an investigator of some sort."

Luke considered the situation, his narrow black eyes fixed on Ripp's face. He told the exact truth. "For several weeks I have been working in the capacity of a Class D Flunky on a tunnel gang."

"What the devil do you investigate on a tunnel gang?" Ripp asked in chilly amusement.

Luke made a slight gesture, one signifying much or nothing, as the other might choose to take it. "Last night the foreman of this gang received a policy directive issued by Lavester Limon of the Office of Procurement. For sheer imbecility this policy caps any of my experience."

"If it's Limon's doings, I can well believe it," said Ripp between his teeth.

"I sought him out in his office. He refused to accept the responsibility and referred me to you."

Ripp sat a trifle straighter in his chair. "What policy is this?"

Luke passed the two directives across the desk. Ripp read slowly, then reluctantly returned the directives. "I fail to see exactly—" He paused. "I should say, these directives merely reflect instructions received by me which I have implemented. Where is the difficulty?"

"Let me cite my personal experience," said Luke. "This morning—as I say, in my temporary capacity as a flunky—I carried a shovel from tunnel head to warehouse and checked it. The operation required an hour and a half. If I were working steadily on a job of this sort, I'd be quite demoralized."

Ripp appeared untroubled. "I can only refer you to my superiors." He spoke aside into his desk phone. "Please transmit File OR nine, Item one-two-three." He turned back to Luke. "I can't take responsibility, either for the directive or for revoking it. May I ask what sort of investigation takes you down into the tunnels? And to whom you report?"

At a loss for words at once evasive and convincing, Luke conveyed an attitude of contemptuous silence.

Judiath Ripp contracted the skin around his blank round eyes in a frown. "As I consider this matter I become increasingly puzzled. Why is this subject a matter for investigation? Just who—"

From a slot appeared the directive Ripp had requested. He glanced at it, then tossed it to Luke. "You'll see that this relieves me totally of responsibility," he said curtly.

The directive was the standard form:

PUBLIC WORKS DEPARTMENT, PUBLIC UTILITIES DIVISION

Office of
The Commissioner of Public Utilities

Policy Directive: 449 Series UA-14-G2
Order Code: GZP—AAR—REF
Reference: TQ9—1422
Date Code: BP—EQ—LLT
Authorized: PU-PUD-Org.
Checked: G. Evan
Counterchecked: Hernon Klanech

From: Parris deVicker, Commissioner of Public Utilities
Through: All District Agencies of Sanitary Works
To: All Department Heads
Attention:

Subject: The urgent need for sharp and immediate economies in the use of equipment and consumption of supplies.

Instant of Application: Immediate
Duration of Relevance: Permanent
Substance: All department heads are instructed to initiate, effect, and enforce rigid economies in the employment of supplies and equipment, especially those items comprised of or manufactured from alloy metals or requiring the functional consumption of same, in those areas in which official authority is exercised. A decrement of 2% will be considered minimal. Status augmentation will in some measure be affected by economies achieved.

Directive reviewed and transmitted: Lee Jon Smith, District Agent of Sanitary Works 8892

56

Luke rose to his feet, concerned now only to depart from the office as quickly as possible. He indicated the directive. "This is a copy?"

"Yes."

"I'll take it, if I may." He included it with the previous two.

Judiath Ripp watched with a faint but definite suspicion. "I fail to understand whom you represent."

"Sometimes the less one knows the better," said Luke.

The suspicion faded from Judiath Ripp's piscine face. Only a person secure in his status could afford to use language of this sort to a member of the low High Echelon. He nodded slightly. "Is that all you require?"

"No," said Luke, "but it's all I can get here."

He turned toward the door, feeling the rake of Ripp's eyes on his back.

Ripp's voice cut at him suddenly and sharply. "Just a moment."

Luke slowly turned.

"Who are you? Let me see your credentials."

Luke laughed coarsely. "I don't have any."

Judiath Ripp rose to his feet, stood towering with knuckles pressed on the desk. Suddenly Luke saw that, after all, Judiath Ripp *was* choleric. His face, mackerel-pale, became suffused with salmon-pink. "Identify yourself," he said throatily, "before I call the watchman."

"Certainly," said Luke. "I have nothing to hide. I am Luke Grogatch. I work as Class D Flunky on Tunnel Gang Number Three, out of the Bureau of Sewer Construction and Maintenance."

"What are you doing here, misrepresenting yourself, wasting my time?"

"Where did I misrepresent myself?" demanded Luke in a contentious voice. "I came here to find out why I had to carry my shovel to the warehouse this morning. It cost me an hour and a half. It doesn't make sense. You've been ordered to economize two per cent, so I spend three hours a day carrying a shovel back and forth."

Judiath Ripp stared at Luke for a few seconds, then abruptly sat down. "You're a Class D Flunky?"

"That's right."

"Hmm. You've been to the Office of Procurement. The manager sent you here?"

"No. He gave me a copy of his directive, just as you did."

The salmon-pink flush had died from Ripp's flat cheeks. The carplike mouth twitched in infinitesimal amusement. "No harm in that, certainly. What do you hope to achieve?"

"I don't want to carry that blasted shovel back and forth. I'd like you to issue orders to that effect."

Judiath Ripp spread his pale mouth in a cold, drooping smile. "Bring me a policy directive to that effect from Parris deVicker and I'll be glad to oblige you. Now—"

"Will you make an appointment for me?"

"An appointment?" Ripp was puzzled. "With whom?"

"With the Commissioner of Public Utilities."

"Pffah!" Ripp waved his hand in cold dismissal. "Get out."

Luke stood in the blue mosaic entry seething with hate for Ripp, Limon, Miskitman, and every intervening functionary. If he were only chairman of the board for a brief two hours (went the oft-repeated daydream), how they'd quickstep! In his mind's eye he saw Judiath Ripp shoveling wads of wet waste with a leaden shovel while a rotary driller, twice as noisy and twice as violent, blew back gales of hot dust and rock chips across his neck. Lavester Limon would be forced to change the smoking teeth of the drill with a small and rusty monkey wrench, while Fedor Miskitman, before and after the shift, carried shovel, monkey wrench, and all the worn teeth to and from the warehouse.

Luke stood moping in the passage for five minutes, then escalated to the surface, which at this point, by virtue of Bramblebury Park, could clearly be distinguishable as the surface and not just another level among coequal levels. He walked slowly along the gravel paths, ignoring the open sky for the immediacy of his problems. He faced a dead end. There was no further scope of action. Judiath Ripp had mockingly suggested that he consult the Commissioner of Public Utilities. Even if by some improbable circumstance he secured an appointment with the Commissioner, what good would ensue? Why should the Commissioner revoke a policy directive of such evident importance? Unless he could be persuaded—by some instrumentality Luke was unable to define or even imagine—to issue a special directive exempting Luke from the provision of the policy . . . Luke chuckled hollowly, a noise which alarmed the pigeons strutting along the walk. Now what? Back to the dormitory. His dormitory privileges included twelve hours' use of his cot per day, and he was not extracting full value from his expense account unless he made use of it. But Luke had no desire for sleep. As he glanced up at the perspective of the towers surrounding the park he felt a melancholy exhilaration. The sky, the wonderful clear open sky, blue and brilliant! Luke shivered, for the sun here was hidden by the Morgenthau Moonspike, and the air was brisk.

Luke crossed the park, thinking to sit where a band of hazy sunlight slashed down between the towers. The benches were crowded with blinking old men and women, but Luke presently found a seat. He sat looking up into the sky, enjoying the mild natural sun warmth. How seldom did he see the sun! In his youth he had frequently set forth on long cross-city hikes, rambling high along the skyways, with space to right and left, the clouds near enough for intimate inspection, the sunlight sparkling and stinging his skin. Gradually the hikes had spread apart, coming at ever longer intervals, and now he could hardly remember when last he'd tramped the wind-lanes. What dreams he had had in those early days, what exuberant visions! Obstacles seemed trivial; he had seen himself clawing up the list, winning a good expense account, the choicest of perquisites, unnumbered Special Coupons! He had planned to have a private air-car, unrestricted nutrition, an apartment far above the surface, high and remote. . . . Dreams. Luke had been victimized by his tongue, his quick temper, his obstinacy. At heart, he was no Nonconformist—no, cried Luke, never! Luke has been born of tycoon stock, and through influence, a word here, a hint there, had been launched into the Organization of a high status. But circumstances and Luke's chronic truculence had driven him into opposition with established ways, and down the Status List he had gone: through professional scholarships, technical trainee appointments, craft apprenticeships, all the varieties of semiskills and machine operation. Now he was Luke Grogatch, flunky, unskilled, Class D, facing the final declassification. But still too vain to carry a shovel. No: Luke corrected himself. His vanity was not at stake. Vanity he had discarded long ago, along with his youthful dreams. All he had left was pride, his right to use the word "I" in connection with himself. If he submitted to Policy Directive 6511 he would relinquish this right; he would be absorbed into the masses of the Organization as a spatter of foam falls back and is absorbed into the ocean. . . . Luke jerked nervously to his feet. He wasted time sitting here. Judiath Ripp, with conger-like malice, had suggested a directive from the Commissioner of Public Utilities. Very well, Luke would obtain that directive and fling it down under Ripp's pale round nostrils.

How?

Luke rubbed his chin dubiously. He walked to a communication booth and checked the directory. As he had surmised, the Commission of Public Utilities was housed in the Organization Central Tower, in Silverado, District 3666, ninety miles to the north.

Luke stood in the watery sunlight, hoping for inspiration. The aged idlers, huddling on the benches like winterbound sparrows, watched him incuriously. Once again Luke was obscurely pleased with his purchase of new clothes. A fine figure he cut, he assured himself.

How? wondered Luke. How to gain an appointment with the Commissioner? How to persuade him to change his views?

No inkling of a solution presented itself.

He looked at his watch: it was still only midmorning. Ample time to visit Organization Central and return in time to report for duty. . . . Luke grimaced wanly. Was his resolution so feeble, then? Was he, after all, to slink back into the tunnel tonight carrying the hated shovel? Luke shook his head slowly. He did not know.

At the Bramblebury Interchange Luke boarded an express highline northbound for Silverado Station. With a hiss and a whine, the shining metal worm darted forward, sliding up to the 13th Level, flashing north at great speed in and out of the sunlight, through tunnels, across chasms between towers, with far below the nervous seethe of the city. Four times the express sighed to a halt: at IBM University, at Braemar, at Great Northern Junction, and finally, thirty minutes out of Bramblebury, at Silverado Central, Luke disembarked; the express slid away through the towers, lithe as an eel through waterweed.

Luke entered the tenth-level foyer of the Central Tower, a vast cave of marble and bronze. Throngs of men and women thrust past him: grim, striding tycoons, stamped with the look of destiny, High Echelon personnel, their assistants, the assistants to their assistants, functionaries on down the list, all dutifully wearing high-status garments, the lesser folk hoping to be mistaken for their superiors. All hurried, tense-faced and abrupt, partly from habit, partly because only a person of low status had no need to hurry. Luke thrust and elbowed with the best of them, and made his way to the central kiosk where he consulted a directory.

Parris deVicker, Commissioner of Public Utilities, had his office on the 59th Level. Luke passed him by and located the Secretary of Public Affairs, Mr. Sowell Sepp, on the 81st Level. No more underlings, thought Luke. This time I'm going to the top. If anyone can resolve this matter, it's Sewell Sepp.

He put himself aboard the lift and emerged into the lobby of the Department of Public Affairs—a splendid place, glittering with disciplined color and ornament after that mock-antique décor known as Second Institutional. The walls were of polished milk glass inset with medallions of shifting kaleidoscopic flashes. The floor was diapered in blue and white sparklestone. A dozen bronze statues dominated the room, massive figures symbolizing the basic public services: communication, transport, education, water, energy, and sanitation. Luke skirted the pedestals and crossed to the reception counter, where ten young women in handsome brown and black uniforms stood with military precision, each to her six feet of counter top. Luke selected one of these girls, who curved her lips in an automatic empty smile.

"Yes, sir?"

"I want to see Mr. Sepp," said Luke brazenly.

The girl's smile remained frozen while she looked at him with startled eyes. "Mr. who?"

"Sewell Sepp, the Secretary of Public Affairs."

The girl asked gently, "Do you have an appointment, sir?"

"No."

"It's impossible, sir."

Luke nodded sourly. "Then I'll see Commissioner Parris deVicker."

"Do you have an appointment to see Mr. deVicker?"

"No, I'm afraid not."

The girl shook her head with a trace of amusement. "Sir, you can't just walk in on these people. They're extremely busy. Everyone must have an appointment."

"Oh, come now," said Luke. "Surely it's conceivable that—"

"Definitely not, sir."

"Then," said Luke, "I'll make an appointment. I'd like to see Mr. Sepp some time today, if possible."

The girl lost interest in Luke. She resumed her manner of impersonal courtesy. "I'll call the office of Mr. Sepp's appointment secretary."

She spoke into a mesh, then turned back to Luke. "No appointments are open this months, sir. Will you speak to someone else? Some under-official?"

"No," said Luke. He gripped the edge of the counter for a moment, started to turn away, then asked, "Who authorizes these appointments?"

"The secretary's first aide, who screens the list of applications."

"I'll speak to the first aide, then."

The girl sighed. "You need an appointment, sir."

"I need an appointment to make an appointment?"

"Yes, sir."

"Do I need an appointment to make an appointment for an appointment?"

62

"No, sir. Just walk right in."

"Where?"

"Suite Forty-two, inside the rotunda, sir."

Luke passed through twelve-foot crystal doors and walked down a short hall. Scurrying patterns of color followed him like shadows along both the walls, grotesque cubistic shapes parodying the motion of his body: a whimsey which surprised Luke and which might have pleased him under less critical circumstances.

He passed through another pair of crystal portals into the rotunda. Six levels above, a domed ceiling depicted scenes of legend in stained glass. Behind a ring of leather couches doors gave into surrounding offices; one of these doors, directly across from the entrance, bore the words:

OFFICES OF THE SECRETARY
DEPARTMENT OF PUBLIC AFFAIRS

On the couches, half a hundred men and women waited with varying degrees of patience. The careful disdain with which they surveyed each other suggested that their status was high; the frequency with which they consulted their watches conveyed the impression that they were momentarily on the point of departure.

A mellow voice sounded over a loudspeaker: "Mr. Artur Coff, please, to the Office of the Secretary." A plump gentleman threw down the periodical he had fretfully been examining and jumped to his feet. He crossed to the bronze and black glass door and passed through.

Luke watched him enviously, then turned aside through an arch marked *Suite 42*. An usher in a brown and black uniform stepped forward: Luke stated his business and was conducted into a small cubicle.

A young man behind a metal desk peered intently at him. "Sit down, please." He motioned to a chair. "Your name?"

"Luke Grogatch."

"Ah, Mr. Grogatch. May I inquire your business?"

"I have something to say to the Secretary of Public Affairs."

"Regarding what subject?"

63

"A personal matter."

"I'm sorry, Mr. Grogatch. The Secretary is more than busy. He's swamped with important Organization business. But if you'll explain the situation to me, I'll recommend you to an appropriate member of the staff."

"That won't help," said Luke. "I want to consult the Secretary in relation to a recently issued policy directive."

"Issued by the Secretary?"

"Yes."

"You wish to object to this directive?"

Luke grudgingly admitted as much.

"There are appropriate channels for this process," said the aide decisively. "If you will fill out this form—not here, but in the rotunda—drop it into the suggestion box to the right of the door as you go out—"

In sudden fury Luke wadded up the form and flung it down on the desk. "Surely he has five minutes free—"

"I'm afraid not, Mr. Grogatch," the aide said in a voice of ice. "If you will look through the rotunda you will see a number of very important people who have waited, some of them for months, for five minutes with the Secretary. If you wish to fill out an application, stating your business in detail, I will see that it receives due consideration."

Luke stalked out of the cubicle. The aide watched him go with a bleak smile of dislike. The man obviously had Nonconformist tendencies, he thought . . . probably should be watched.

Luke stood in the rotunda, muttering, "What now? What now? What now?" in a half-mesmerized undertone. He stared around the rotunda, at the pompous High Echelon folk, arrogantly consulting their watches and tapping their feet. "Mr. Jepper Prinn!" called the mellow voice over the loudspeaker. "The Office of the Secretary, if you please." Luke watched Jepper Prinn walk to the bronze and black glass portal.

Luke slumped into a chair, scratched his long nose, looked cautiously around the rotunda. Nearby sat a big, bull-necked man with a red face, protruding lips, a shock of rank blond hair—a tycoon, judging from his air of absolute authority.

Luke rose and went to a desk placed for the convenience of those waiting. He took several sheets of paper with the Tower letterhead and unobtrusively circled the rotunda to the entrance into Suite 42. The bull-necked tycoon paid him no heed.

Luke girded himself, closing his collar, adjusting the set of his jacket. He took a deep breath, then, when the florid man glanced in his direction, came forward officiously. He looked briskly around the circle of couches, consulting his papers; then catching the eye of the tycoon, frowned, squinted, walked forward.

"Your name, sir?" asked Luke in an official voice.

"I'm Hardin Arthur," rasped the tycoon. "Why?"

Luke nodded, consulted his paper. "The time of your appointment?"

"Eleven-ten. What of it?"

"The Secretary would like to know if you can conveniently lunch with him at one-thirty?"

Arthur considered. "I suppose it's possible," he grumbled. "I'll have to rearrange some other business. . . . An inconvenience—but I can do it, yes."

"Excellent," said Luke. "At lunch the Secretary feels that he can discuss your business more informally and at greater length than at eleven-ten, when he can only allow you seven minutes."

"Seven minutes!" rumbled Arthur indignantly. "I can hardly spread my plans out in seven minutes."

"Yes, sir," said Luke. "The Secretary realizes this, and suggests that you lunch with him."

Arthur petulantly hauled himself to his feet. "Very well. Lunch at one-thirty, correct?"

"Correct, sir. If you will walk directly into the Secretary's office at that time."

Arthur departed the rotunda, and Luke settled into the seat Arthur had vacated.

Time passed very slowly. At ten minutes after eleven the mellow voice called out, "Mr. Hardin Arthur, please. To the Office of the Secretary."

Luke rose to his feet, stalked with great dignity across the rotunda, and went through the bronze and black glass door.

Behind a long black desk sat the Secretary, a rather un-distinguished man with gray hair and snapping gray eyes. He raised his eyebrows as Luke came forward: Luke evidently did not fit his preconception of Hardin Arthur.

The Secretary spoke. "Sit down, Mr. Arthur. I may as well tell you bluntly and frankly that we think your scheme is impractical. By 'we' I mean myself and the Board of Policy Evaluation—who of course have referred to the Files. First, the costs are excessive. Second, there's no guarantee that you can phase your program into that of our other tycoons. Third, the Board of Policy Evaluation tells me that Files doubts whether we'll need that much new capacity."

"Ah," Luke nodded wisely. "I see. Well, no matter. It's not important."

"Not important?" The Secretary sat up in his chair, stared at Luke in wonder. "I'm surprised to hear you say so."

Luke made an airy gesture. "Forget it. Life's too short to worry about these things. Actually there's another matter I want to discuss with you."

"Ah?"

"It may seem trivial, but the implications are large. A former employee called the matter to my attention. He's now a flunky on one of the sewer maintenance tunnel gangs, an excellent chap. Here's the situation. Some idiotic jack-in-office has issued a directive which forces this man to carry a shovel back and forth to the warehouse every day, before and after work. I've taken the trouble to follow up the matter and the chain leads here." He displayed his three policy directives.

Frowning, the Secretary glanced through them. "These all seem perfectly regular. What do you want me to do?"

"Issue a directive clarifying the policy. After all, we can't have these poor devils working three hours overtime for tomfoolishness."

"Tomfoolishness?" The Secretary was displeased. "Hardly that, Mr. Arthur. The economy directive came to me from the Board of Directors, from the Chairman himself, and if—"

"Don't mistake me," said Luke hastily. "I've no quarrel
66

with economy; I merely want the policy applied sensibly. Checking a shovel into the warehouse—where's the economy in that?"

"Multiply that shovel by a million, Mr. Arthur," said the Secretary coldly.

"Very well, multiply it," argued Luke. "We have a million shovels. How many of these million shovels are conserved by this order? Two or three a year?"

The Secretary shrugged. "Obviously in a general directive of this sort, inequalities occur. So far as I'm concerned, I issued the directive because I was instructed to do so. If you want it changed you'll have to consult the Chairman of the Board."

"Very well. Can you arrange an appointment for me?"

"Let's settle the matter even sooner," said the Secretary. "Right now. We'll talk to him across the screen, although, as you say, it seems a trivial matter. . . ."

"Demoralization of the working force isn't trivial, Secretary Sepp."

The Secretary shrugged, touched a button, spoke into a mesh. "The Chairman of the Board, if he's not occupied."

The screen glowed. The Chairman of the Board of Directors looked out at them. He sat in a lounge chair on the deck of his penthouse at the pinnacle of the tower. In one hand he held a glass of pale effervescent liquid; beyond him opened sunlight and blue air and a wide glimpse of the miraculous city.

"Good morning, Sepp," said the Chairman cordially, and nodded toward Luke. "Good morning to you, sir."

"Chairman, Mr. Arthur here is protesting the economy directive you sent down a few days ago. He claims that strict application is causing hardship among the labor force: demoralization, actually. Something to do with shovels."

The Chairman considered. "Economy directive? I hardly recall the exact case."

Secretary Sepp described the directive, citing code and reference numbers, explaining the provisions, and the Chairman nodded in recollection. "Yes, the metal shortage thing. Afraid I can't help you, Sepp, or you, Mr. Arthur. Policy Evaluation sent it up. Apparently we're

67

running short of minerals; what else can we do? Cinch in the old belts, eh? Hard on all of us. What's this about shovels?"

"It's the whole matter," cried Luke in sudden shrillness, evoking startled glances from Secretary and Chairman. "Carrying a shovel back and forth to the warehouse—three hours a day! It's not economy, it's a disorganized farce!"

"Come now, Mr. Arthur," the Chairman chided humorously. "So long as you're not carrying the shovel yourself, why the excitement? It works the very devil with one's digestion. Until Policy Evaluation changes its collective mind—as it often does—then we've got to string along. Can't go counter to Policy Evaluation, you know. They're the people with the facts and figures."

"Neither here nor there," mumbled Luke. "Carrying a shovel three hours—"

"Perhaps a bit of bother for the men concerned," said the Chairman with a hint of impatience, "but they've got to see the thing from the long view. Sepp, perhaps you'll lunch with me? A marvelous day, lazy weather."

"Thank you, Mr. Chairman. I'll be pleased indeed."

"Excellent. At one or one-thirty, whenever it's convenient for you."

The screen went blank. Secretary Sepp rose to his feet. "There it is, Mr. Arthur. I can't do any more."

"Very well, Mr. Secretary," said Luke in a hollow voice.

"Sorry I can't be of more help in that other matter, but as I say—"

"It's inconsequential."

Luke turned, left the elegant office, passed through the bronze and black glass doors into the rotunda. Through the arch into Suite 42 he saw a large, bull-necked man, tomato-red in the face, hunched forward across a counter. Luke stepped forward smartly, leaving the rotunda just as the authentic Mr. Arthur and the aide came forth, deep in agitated conversation.

Luke stopped by the information desk. "Where is the Policy Evaluation Board?"

"Twenty-ninth Level, sir, this building."

In Policy Evaluation on the 29th Level Luke talked with a silk-mustached young man, courtly and elegant, with the status classification Plan Coordinator. "Certainly!" exclaimed the young man in response to Luke's question. Authoritative information is the basis of authoritative organization. Material from Files is collated and digested in the Bureau of Abstracts, and sent up to us. We shape it and present it to the Board of Directors in the form of a daily précis."

Luke expressed interest in the Bureau of Abstracts, and the young man quickly became bored. "Grubbers among the statistics, barely able to compose an intelligible sentence. If it weren't for us . . ." His eyebrows, silken as his mustache, hinted of the disasters which in the absence of Policy Evaluation would overtake the Organization. "They work in a suite down on the Sixth Level."

Luke descended to the Bureau of Abstracts, and found no difficulty gaining admission to the general office. In contrast to the rather nebulous intellectualism of Policy Evaluation, the Bureau of Abstracts seemed workaday and matter-of-fact. A middle-aged woman, cheerfully fat, inquired Luke's business, and when Luke professed himself a journalist, conducted him about the premises. They went from the main lobby, walled in antique cream-colored plaster with gold scrollwork, past the fusty cubicles, where clerks sat at projection-desks, scanning ribbons of words. Extracting idea-sequence, emending excising, condensing, cross-referring, finally producing the abstract to be submitted to Policy Evaluation. Luke's fat and cheerful guide brewed them a pot of tea; she asked questions which Luke answered in general terms, straining his voice and pursing his mouth in the effort to seem agreeable and hearty. He himself asked questions.

"I'm interested in a set of statistics on the scarcity of metals, or ores, or something similar, which recently went up to Policy Evaluation. Would you know anything about this?"

"Heavens, no!" the woman responded. "There's just too much material coming in—the business of the entire Organization."

"Where does this material come from? Who sends it to you?"

The woman made a humorous little grimace of distaste. "From Files, down on Sublevel Twelve. I can't tell you much, because we don't associate with the personnel. They're low status: clerks and the like. Sheer automatons."

Luke expressed an interest in the source of the Bureau of Abstract's information. The woman shrugged, as if to say, everyone to his own taste. "I'll call down to the Chief File Clerk; I know him, very slightly."

The Chief File Clerk, Mr. Sidd Boatridge, was self-important and brusque, as if aware of the low esteem in which he was held by the Bureau of Abstracts. He dismissed Luke's questions with a stony face of indifference. "I really have no idea, sir. We file, index, and cross-index material into the Information Bank, but we concern ourselves very little with outgoing data. My duties in fact are mainly administrative. I'll call in one of the under-clerks; he can tell you more than I can."

The under-clerk who answered Boatridge's summons was a short, turnip-faced man with matted red hair. "Take Mr. Grogatch into the outer office," said the Chief File Clerk testily. "He wants to ask you a few questions."

In the outer office, out of the Chief File Clerk's hearing, the under-clerk became rather surly and pompous, as if he had divined the level of Luke's status. He referred to himself as a "line-tender" rather than as a file clerk, the latter apparently being a classification of lesser prestige. His "line-tending" consisted of sitting beside a panel which glowed and blinked with a thousand orange and green lights. "The orange lights indicate information going down into the Bank," said the file clerk. "The green lights show where somebody up-level is drawing information out—generally at the Bureau of Abstracts."

Luke observed the orange and green flickers for a moment. "What information is being transmitted now?"

"Couldn't say," the file clerk grunted. "It's all coded. Down in the old office we had a monitoring machine and never used it. Too much else to do."

Luke considered. The file clerk showed signs of restiveness. Luke's mind worked hurriedly. He asked, "So—as I understand it—you file information, but have nothing further to do with it?"

"We file it and code it. Whoever wants information puts a program into the works and the information goes out to him. We never see it, unless we go and look in the old monitoring machine."

"Which is still down at your old office?"

The file clerk nodded. "They call it the staging chamber now. Nothing there but input and output pipes, the monitor, and the custodian."

"Where is the staging chamber?"

"Way down the levels, behind the Bank. Too low for me to work. I got more ambition." For emphasis he spat on the floor.

"A custodian is there, you say?"

"An old junior executive named Dodkin. He s been there a hundred years."

Luke dropped thirty levels aboard an express lift, then rode the down escalator another six levels to Sublevel 46. He emerged on a dingy landing with a low-perquisite nutrition hall to one side, a life attendant's dormitory to the other. The air carried the familiar reek of the deep underground, a compound of dank concrete, phenol, mercaptans, and a discreet but pervasive human smell. Luke realized with bitter amusement that he had returned to familiar territory.

Following instructions grudgingly detailed by the under-file clerk, Luke stepped aboard a chattering man-belt labeled 902—Tanks. Presently he came to a brightly lit landing marked by a black and yellow sign: INFORMATION TANKS. TECHNICAL STATION. Inside the door a number of mechanics sat on stools, dangling their legs, lounging, chaffering.

Luke changed to a side-belt, even more dilapidated, almost in a state of disrepair. At the second junction—this one unmarked—he left the man-belt and turned down a narrow passage toward a far yellow bulb. The passage was silent, almost sinister in its dissociation from the life of the city.

Below the single yellow bulb a dented metal door was daubed with a sign:

INFORMATION TANKS—STAGING CHAMBER
NO ADMITTANCE

Luke tested the door and found it locked. He rapped and waited.

Silence shrouded the passage, broken only by a faint sound from the distant man-belt.

Luke rapped again, and now from within came a shuffle of movement. The door slid back and a pale placid eye looked forth. A rather weak voice inquired, "Yes, sir?"

Luke attempted a manner of easy authority. "You're Dodkin the custodian?"

"Yes, sir, I'm Dodkin."

"Open up, please. I'd like to come in."

The pale eye blinked in mild wonder. "This is only the staging room, sir. There's nothing here to see. The storage complexes are around to the front; if you'll go back to the junction—"

Luke broke into the flow of words. "I've just come down from the Files; it's you I want to see."

The pale eye blinked once more; the door slid open. Luke entered the long, narrow, concrete-floored staging room. Conduits dropped from the ceiling by the thousands, bent, twisted, and looped, and entered the wall, each conduit labeled with a dangling metal tag. At one end of the room was a grimy cot where Dodkin apparently slept; at the other end was a long black desk: the monitoring machine? Dodkin himself was small and stooped, but moved nimbly in spite of his evident age. His white hair was stained but well brushed; his gaze, weak and watery, was without guile, and fixed on Luke with an astronomer's detachment. He opened his mouth, and words quavered forth in spate, with Luke vainly seeking to interrupt.

"Not often do visitors come from above. Is something wrong?"

"No, nothing wrong."

72

"They should tell me if aught isn't correct, or perhaps there's been new policies of which I haven't been notified."

"Nothing like that, Mr. Dodkin. I'm just a visitor—"

"I don't move out as much as I used to, but last week I—"

Luke pretended to listen while Dodkin maundered on in obbligato to Luke's bitter thoughts. The continuity of directives leading from Fedor Miskitman to Lavester Limon to Judiath Ripp, bypassing Parris deVicker to Sewell Sepp and the Chairman of the Board, then returning down the classifications, down the levels, through the Policy Evaluation Board, the Bureau of Abstracts, the File Clerk's Office—the continuity had finally ended; the thread he had traced with such forlorn hope seemed about to lose itself. Well, Luke told himself, he had accepted Miskitman's challenge; he had failed, and now was faced with his original choice. Submit, carry the wretched shovel back and forth to the warehouse, or defy the order, throw down his shovel, assert himself as a free-willed man, and be declassified, to become a junior executive like old Dodkin—who, sucking and wheezing, still rambled on in compulsive loquacity.

". . . Something incorrect, I'd never know, because who ever tells me? From year end to year end I'm quiet down here, and there's no one to relieve me, and I only get to the up-side rarely, once a fortnight or so, but then once you've seen the sky, does it ever change? And the sun, the marvel of it, but once you've seen a marvel—"

Luke drew a deep breath. "I'm investigating an item of information which reached the File Clerk's Office. I wonder if you can help me."

Dodkin blinked his pale eyes. "What item is this, sir? Naturally I'll be glad to help in any way, even though—"

"The item dealt with economy in the use of metals and metal tools."

Dodkin nodded. "I remember them perfectly."

It was Luke's turn to stare. "You *remember* this item?"

"Certainly. It was, if I may say so, one of my little interpolations. A personal observation which I included among the other material."

"Would you be kind enough to explain?"

73

Dodkin would be only too pleased to explain. "Last week I had occasion to visit an old friend over by Claxton Abbey, a fine conformist, well adapted and cooperative, even if, alas, like myself, a junior executive. Of course, I mean no disrespect to good Davy Evans, like myself about ready for the pension—though little enough they allow nowadays—"

"The interpolation?"

"Yes, indeed. On my way home along the man-belt—on Sublevel Thirty-two, as I recall—I saw a workman of some sort—perhaps an electrical technician—toss several tools into a crevice on his way off-shift. I thought, now there's a slovenly act—disgraceful! Suppose the man forgot where he had hidden his tools? They'd be lost! Our reserves of raw metallic ore are very low—that's common knowledge—and every year the ocean water becomes weaker and more dilute. That man had no regard for the future of Organization. We should cherish our natural resources, do you not agree, sir?"

"I agree, naturally. But—"

"In any event, I returned here and added a memorandum to that effect into the material which goes up to the Assistant File Clerk. I thought that perhaps he'd be impressed and say a word to someone with influence—perhaps the Head File Clerk. In any event, there's the tale of my interpolation. Naturally I attempted to give it weight by citing the inevitable diminution of our natural resources."

"I see," said Luke. "And do you frequently include interpolations into the day's information?"

"Occasionally," said Dodkin, "and sometimes, I'm glad to say, people more important than I share my views. Only three weeks ago I was delayed several minutes on my way between Claxton Abbey and Kittsville on Sublevel Thirty. I made a note of it, and last week I noticed that construction has commenced on a new eight-lane man-belt between the two points, a really magnificent and modern undertaking. A month ago I noticed a shameless group of girls daubed like savages with cosmetic. What a waste, I told myself; what vanity and folly! I hinted as much in a little message to the Under-File Clerk. I seem

74

to be just one of the many with these views, for two days later a general order discouraging these petty vanities was issued by the Secretary of Education."

"Interesting," Luke muttered. "Interesting indeed. How do you include these—interpolations—into the information?"

Dodkin hobbled nimbly to the monitoring machine. "The output from the tanks comes through here. I print a bit on the typewriter and tuck it where the Under-Clerk will see it."

"Admirable," sighed Luke. "A man with your intelligence should have ranked higher in the Status List."

Dodkin shook his placid old head. "I don't have the ambition nor the ability. I'm fit for just this simple job, and that only barely. I'd take my pension tomorrow, only the Chief File Clerk asked me to stay on a bit until he could find a man to take my place. No one seems to like the quiet down here."

"Perhaps you'll have your pension sooner than you think," said Luke.

Luke strolled along the glossy tube, ringed with alternate pale and dark refractions like a bull's-eye. Ahead was motion, the glint of metal, the mutter of voices. The entire crew of Tunnel Gang Number 3 stood idle and restless.

Fedor Miskitman waved his arm with uncharacteristic vehemence. "Grogatch! At your post! You've held up the entire crew!" His heavy face was suffused with pink. "Four minutes already we're behind schedule."

Luke strolled closer.

"Hurry!" bellowed Miskitman. "What do you think this is, a blasted promenade?"

If anything, Luke slackened his pace. Fedor Miskitman lowered his big head, staring balefully. Luke halted in front of him.

"Where's your shovel?" Fedor Miskitman asked.

"I don't know," said Luke. "I'm here on the job. It's up to you to provide tools."

Fedor Miskitman stared unbelievingly. "Didn't you take it to the warehouse?"

75

"Yes," said Luke. "I took it there. If you want it go get it—"

Fedor Miskitman opened his mouth. He roared, "Get off the job!"

"Just as you like," said Luke. "You're the foreman."

"Don't come back!" bellowed Miskitman. "I'll report you before the day is out. You won't gain status from me, I tell you that!"

"Status?" Luke laughed. "Go ahead. Cut me down to junior executive. Do you think I care? No. And I'll tell you why. There's going to be a change or two made. When things seem different to you, think of me."

Luke Grogatch, Junior Executive, said good-bye to the retiring custodian of the staging chamber. "Don't thank me, not at all," said Luke. "I'm here by my own doing. In fact—well, never mind all that. Go up-side, sit in the sun, enjoy the air."

Finally Dodkin, in mingled joy and sorrow, hobbled for the last time down the musty passageway to the chattering man-belt.

Luke was alone in the staging chamber. Around him hummed the near-inaudible rush of information. From behind the wall came the sense of a million relays clicking, twitching, meshing; of cylinders and trace-tubes and memory-lakes whirring with activity. At the monitoring machine the output streamed forth on a reel of yellow tape. Nearby rested the typewriter.

Luke seated himself. His first interpolation: what should it be? Freedom for the Nonconformists? Tunnel gang foreman to carry tools for the entire crew? A higher expense account for junior executives?

Luke rose to his feet and scratched his chin. Power . . . to be subtly applied. How should he use it? To secure rich perquisites for himself? Yes, of course, this he would accomplish, by devious means. And then—what? Luke thought of the billions of men and women living, and working in the Organization. He looked at the typewriter. He could shape their lives, change their thoughts, disorganize the Organization. Was this wise? Or right? Or even amusing?

Luke sighed. In his mind's eye he saw himself standing on a high terrace overlooking the city. Luke Grogatch, Chairman of the Board. Not impossible, quite feasible. A little at a time, the correct interpolations . . . Luke Grogatch, Chairman of the Board. Yes. This for a starter. But it was necessary to move cautiously, with great delicacy.

Luke seated himself at the typewriter and began to pick out his first interpolation.

ULLWARD'S RETREAT

Bruham Ullward had invited three friends to lunch at his ranch: Ted and Ravelin Seehoe, and their adolescent daughter, Iguenae. After an eye-bulging feast, Ullward offered around a tray of the digestive pastilles which had won him his wealth.

"A wonderful meal," said Ted Seehoe reverently. "Too much, really. I'll need one of these. The algae was absolutely marvelous."

Ullward made a smiling, easy gesture. "It's the genuine stuff."

Ravelin Seehoe, a fresh-faced, rather positive young woman of eighty of ninety, reached for a pastille. "A shame there's not more of it. The synthetic we get is hardly recognizable as algae."

"It's a problem," Ullward admitted. "I clubbed up with some friends; we bought a little mat in the Ross Sea and grow all our own."

"Think of that," exclaimed Ravelin. "Isn't it frightfully expensive?"

Ullward pursued his lips whimsically. "The good things in life come high. Luckily, I'm able to afford a bit extra."

"What I keep telling Ted—" began Ravelin, then stopped as Ted turned her a keen warning glance.

Ullward bridged the rift. "Money isn't everything. I have a flat of algae, my ranch; you have your daughter—and I'm sure you wouldn't trade."

Ted patted Iugenae's hand. "When do you have your own child, Lamster Ullward?" *(Lamster: Contraction of Landmaster—the polite form of address in current use.)*

78

"Still some time yet. I'm thirty-seven billion down the list."

"A pity," said Ravelin Seehoe brightly, "when you could give a child so many advantages."

"Some day, some day, before I'm too old."

"A shame," said Ravelin, "but it has to be. Another fifty billion people and we'd have no privacy whatever!" She looked admiringly around the room, which was used for the sole purpose of preparing food and dining.

Ullward put his hands on the arms of his chair, hitched forward a little. "Perhaps you'd like to look around the ranch?" He spoke in a casual voice, glancing from one to the other.

Iugenae clapped her hands; Revelin beamed. "If it wouldn't be too much trouble!"

"Oh, we'd love to, Lamster Ullward!" cried Iugenae.

"I've always wanted to see your ranch," said Ted. "I've heard so much about it."

"It's an opportunity for Iugenae I wouldn't want her to miss," said Ravelin. She shook her finger at Iugenae. "Remember, Miss Puss, notice everything very carefully—and don't *touch!*"

"May I take pictures, Mother?"

"You'll have to ask Lamster Ullward."

"Of course, of course," said Ullward. "Why in the world not?" He rose to his feet—a man of more than middle stature, more than middle pudginess, with straight sandy hair, round blue eyes, a prominent beak of a nose. Almost three hundred years old, he guarded his health with great zeal, and looked little more than two hundred.

He stepped to the door, checked the time, touched a dial on the wall. "Are you ready?"

"Yes, we're quite ready," said Ravelin.

Ullward snapped back the wall, to reveal a view over a sylvan glade. A fine oak tree shaded a pond growing with rushes. A path led through a field toward a wooden valley a mile in the distance.

"Magnificent," said Ted. "Simply magnificent!"

They stepped outdoors into the sunlight. Iugenae flung her arms out, twirled, danced in a circle. "Look! I'm all alone. I'm out here all by myself!"

"Iugenae!" called Ravelin sharply. "Be careful! Stay on the path! That's real grass and you mustn't damage it."

Iugenae ran ahead to the pond. "Mother!" she called back. "Look at these funny little jumpy things! And look at the flowers!"

"The animals are frogs," said Ullward. "They have a very interesting life history. You see the little fishlike things in the water?"

"Aren't they funny! Mother, do come here!"

"Those are called tadpoles and they will presently become frogs, indistinguishable from the ones you see."

Ravelin and Ted advanced with more dignity, but were as interested as Iugenae in the frogs.

"Smell the fresh air," Ted told Ravelin. "You'd think you were back in the early times."

"It's absolutely exquisite," said Ravelin. She looked around her. "One has the feeling of being able to wander on and on and on."

"Come around over here," called Ullward from beyond the pool. "This is the rock garden."

In awe, the guests stared at the ledge of rock, stained with red and yellow lichen, tufted with green moss. Ferns grew from a crevice; there were several fragile clusters of white flowers.

Smell the flowers, if you wish," Ullward told Iugenae. "But please don't touch them; they stain rather easily."

Iugenae sniffed. "Mmmm!"

"Are they real?" asked Ted.

"The moss, yes. That clump of ferns and these little succulents are real. The flowers were designed for me by a horticulturist and are exact replicas of certain ancient species. We've actually improved on the odor."

"Wonderful, wonderful," said Ted.

"Now come this way—no, don't look back; I want you to get the total effect . . ." An expression of vexation crossed his face.

"What's the trouble?" asked Ted.

"It's a damned nuisance," said Ullward. "Hear that sound?"

Ted became aware of a faint rolling rumble, deep and almost unheard. "Yes. Sounds like some sort of factory."

"It is. On the floor below. A rug-works. One of the looms creates this terrible row. I've complained, but they pay no attention . . . Oh, well, ignore it. Now stand over here—and look around!"

His friends gasped in rapture. The view from this angle was of a rustic bungalow in an Alpine valley, the door being the opening into Ullward's dining room.

"What an illusion of distance!" exclaimed Ravelin. "A person would almost think he was alone."

"A beautiful piece of work," said Ted. "I'd swear I was looking into ten miles—at least five miles—of distance."

"I've got a lot of space here," said Ullward proudly. "Almost three-quarters of an acre. Would you like to see it by moonlight?"

"Oh, could we?"

Ullward went to a concealed switch-panel; the sun seemed to race across the sky. A fervent glow of sunset lit the valley; the sky burned peacock blue, gold, green, then came twilight—and the rising full moon came up behind the hill.

"This is absolutely marvelous," said Ravelin softly. "How can you bring yourself to leave it?"

"It's hard," admitted Ullward. "But I've got to look after business too. More money, more space."

He turned a knob; the moon floated across the sky, sank. Stars appeared, forming the age-old patterns. Ullward pointed out the constellations and the first-magnitude stars by name, using a penciltorch for a pointer. Then the sky flushed with lavender and lemon yellow and the sun appeared once more. Unseen ducts sent a current of cool air through the glade.

"Right now I'm negotiating for an area behind this wall here." He tapped at the depicted mountainside, an illusion given reality and three-dimensionality by laminations inside the pane. "It's quite a large area—over a hundred square feet. The owner wants a fortune, naturally."

"I'm surprised he wants to sell," said Ted. "A hundred square feet means real privacy."

"There's been a death in the family," explained Ullward. "The owner's four-great-grandfather passed on and the space is temporarily surplus."

Ted nodded. "I hope you're able to get it."

"I hope so too. I've got rather flamboyant ambitions—eventually I hope to own the entire quarterblock—but it takes time. People don't like to sell their space and everyone is anxious to buy."

"Not we," said Ravelin cheerfully. "We have our little home. We're snug and cozy and we're putting money aside for investment."

"Wise," agreed Ullward. "A great many people are space-poor. Then when a chance to make real money comes up, they're undercapitalized. Until I scored with the digestive pastilles, I lived in a single rented locker. I was cramped—but I don't regret it today."

They returned through the glade toward Ullward's house, stopping at the oak tree. "This is my special pride," said Ullward. "A genuine oak tree!"

"Genuine?" asked Ted in astonishment. "I assumed it was simulation."

"So many people do," said Ullward. "No, it's genuine."

"Take a picture of the tree, Iugenae, please. But don't touch it. You might damage the bark."

"Perfectly all right to touch the bark," assured Ullward.

He looked up into the branches, then scanned the ground. He stooped, picked up a fallen leaf. "This grew on the tree," he said. "Now, Iugenae, I want you to come with me." He went to the rock garden, pulled a simulated rock aside, to reveal a cabinet with washbasin. "Watch carefully." He showed her the leaf. "Notice? It's dry and brittle and brown."

"Yes, Lamster Ullward." Iugenae craned her neck.

"First I dip it in this solution." He took a beaker full of dark liquid from a shelf. "So. That restores the green color. We wash off the excess, then dry it. Now we rub this next fluid carefully into the surface. Notice, it's flexible and strong now. One more solution—a plastic coating—and there we are, a true oak leaf, perfectly genuine. It's yours."

82

"Oh, Lamster Ullward! Thank you ever so much!" She ran off to show her father and mother, who were standing by the pool, luxuriating in the feeling of space, watching the frogs. "See what Lamster Ullward gave me!"

"You be very careful with it," said Ravelin. "When we get home, we'll find a nice little frame and you can hang it in your locker."

The simulated sun hung in the western sky. Ullward led the group to a sundial. "An antique, countless years old. Pure marble, carved by hand. It works too—entirely functional. Notice. Three-fifteen by the shadow on the dial . . ." He peered at his beltwatch, squinted at the sun. "Excuse me one moment." He ran to the control board, made an adjustment. The sun lurched ten degrees across the sky. Ullward returned, checked the sundial. "That's better. Notice. Three-fifty by the sundial, three-fifty by my watch. Isn't that something now?"

"It's wonderful," said Ravelin earnestly.

"It's the loveliest thing I've ever seen," chirped Iugenae.

Ravelin looked around the ranch, sighed wistfully. "We hate to leave, but I think we must be returning home."

"It's been a wonderful day, Lamster Ullward," said Ted. "A wonderful lunch, and we enjoyed seeing your ranch."

"You'll have to come out again," invited Ullward. "I always enjoy company."

He led them into the dining room, through the living room-bedroom to the door. The Seehoe family took a last look across the spacious interior, pulled on their mantles, stepped into their run-shoes, made their farewells. Ullward slid back the door. The Seehoes looked out, waited till a gap appeared in the traffic. They waved good-bye, pulled the hoods over their heads, stepped out into the corridor.

The run-shoes spun them toward their home, selecting the appropriate turnings, sliding automatically into the correct lift and drop-pits. Deflection fields twisted them through the throngs. Like the Seehoes, everyone wore mantle and hood of filmy reflective stuff to safeguard privacy. The illusion-pane along the ceiling of the corridor presented a view of towers dwindling up into a cheerful blue sky, as if the pedestrian were moving along one of the windy upper passages.

The Seehoes approached their home. Two hundred yards away, they angled over to the wall. If the flow of traffic carried them past, they would be forced to circle the block and make another attempt to enter. Their door slid open as they spun near; they ducked into the opening, swinging around on a metal grab-bar.

They removed their mantles and run-shoes, sliding skillfully past each other. Iugenae pivoted into the bathroom and there was room for both Ted and Ravelin to sit down. The house was rather small for the three of them; they could well have used another twelve square feet, but rather than pay exorbitant rent, they preferred to save the money with an eye toward Iugenae's future.

Ted sighed in satisfaction, stretching his legs luxuriously under Ravelin's chair. "Ullward's ranch notwithstanding, it's nice to be home."

Iugenae backed out of the bathroom.

Ravelin looked up. "It's time for your pill, dear."

Iugenae screwed up her face. "Oh, Mama! Why do I have to take pills? I feel perfectly well."

"They're good for you, dear."

Iugenae sullenly took a pill from the dispenser. "Runy says you make us take pills to keep us from growing up."

Ted and Ravelin exchanged glances.

"Just take your pill," said Ravelin, "and never mind what Runy says."

"But how is it that I'm 38 and Ermara Burk's only 32 and she's got a figure and I'm like a slat?"

"No arguments, dear. Take your pill."

Ted jumped to his feet. "Here, Babykin, sit down."

Iugenae protested, but Ted held up his hand. "I'll sit in the niche. I've got a few calls that I have to make."

He sidled past Ravelin, seated himself in the niche in front of the communication screen. The illusion-pane behind him was custom-built—Ravelin, in fact, had designed it herself. It simulated a merry little bandit's den, the walls draped in red and yellow silk, a bowl of fruit on the rustic table, a guitar on the bench, a copper teakettle simmering on the countertop stove. The pane had been

84

rather expensive, but when anyone communicated with the Seehoes, it was the first thing they saw, and here the house-proud Ravelin had refused to stint.

Before Ted could make his call, the signal light flashed. He answered; the screen opened to display his friend Loren Aigle, apparently sitting in an airy arched rotunda, against a background of fleecy clouds—an illusion which Ravelin had instantly recognized as an inexpensive stock effect.

Loren and Elme, his wife, were anxious to hear of the Seehoes' visit to the Ullward ranch. Ted described the afternoon in detail. "Space, space, and more space! Isolation pure and simple! Absolute privacy! You can hardly imagine it! A fortune in illusion-panes."

"Nice," said Loren Aigle. "I'll tell you one you'll find hard to believe. Today I registered a whole planet to a man." Loren worked in the Certification Bureau of the Extraterrestrial Properties Agency.

Ted was puzzled and uncomprehending. "A whole planet? How so?"

Loren explained. "He's a free-lance spaceman. Still a few left."

"But what's he planning to do with an entire planet?"

"Live there, he claims."

"Alone?"

Loren nodded. "I had quite a chat with him. Earth is all very well, he says, but he prefers the privacy of his own planet. Can you imagine that?"

"Frankly, no! I can't imagine the fourth dimension either. What a marvel, though!"

The conversation ended and the screen faded. Ted swung around to his wife. "Did you hear that?"

Ravelin nodded; she had heard but not heeded. She was reading the menu supplied by the catering firm to which they subscribed. "We won't want anything heavy after that lunch. They've got simulated synthetic algae again."

Ted grunted. "It's never as good as the genuine synthetic."

"But it's cheaper and we've all had an enormous lunch."

"Don't worry about me, Mom!" sang Iugenae. "I'm going out with Runy."

"Oh, you are, are you? And where are you going, may I ask?"

"A ride around the world. We're catching the seven o'clock shuttle, so I've got to hurry."

"Come right home afterward," said Ravelin severely. "Don't go anywhere else."

"For heaven's sake, Mother, you'd think I was going to elope or something."

"Mind what I say, Miss Puss. I was a girl once myself. Have you taken your medicine?"

"Yes, I've taken my medicine."

Iugenae departed; Ted slipped back into the niche. "Who are you calling now?" asked Ravelin.

"Lamster Ullward. I want to thank him for going to so much trouble for us."

Ravelin agreed that an algae-and-margarine call was no more than polite.

Ted called, expressed his thanks, then—almost as an afterthought—chanced to mention the man who owned a planet.

"An entire planet?" inquired Ullward. "It must be inhabited."

"No, I understand not, Lamster Ullward. Think of it! Think of the privacy!"

"Privacy!" exclaimed Ullward bluffly. "My dear fellow, what do you call this?"

"Oh, naturally, Lamster Ullward—you have a real showplace."

"The planet must be very primitive," Ullward reflected. "An engaging idea, of course—if you like that kind of thing. Who is this man?"

"I don't now, Lamster Ullward. I could find out, if you like."

"No, no, don't bother. I'm not particularly interested. Just an idle thought." Ullward laughed his hearty laugh. "Poor man. Probably lives in a dome."

"That's possible, of course, Lamster Ullward. Well, thanks again, and good night."

The spaceman's name was Kennes Mail. He was short and thin, tough as synthetic herring, brown as toasted yeast. He had a close-cropped pad of gray hair, a keen, if ingenuous, blue gaze. He showed a courteous interest in Ullward's ranch, but Ullward thought his recurrent use of the word "clever" rather tactless.

As they returned to the house, Ullward paused to admire his oak tree.

"It's absolutely genuine, Lamster Mail! A living tree, survival of past ages! Do you have trees as fine as that on your planet?"

Kennes Mail smiled. "Lamster Ullward, that's just a shrub. Let's sit somewhere and I'll show you photographs."

Ullward had already mentioned his interest in acquiring extraterrestrial property; Mail, admitting that he needed money, had given him to understand that some sort of deal might be arranged. They sat at a table; Mail opened his case. Ullward switched on the wallscreen.

"First I'll show you a map," said Mail. He selected a rod, dropped into the table socket. On the wall appeared a world projection: oceans, an enormous equatorial landmass named Gaea; the smaller subcontinents Atalanta, Persephone, Alcyone. A box of descriptive information read:

MAIL'S PLANET

Claim registered and endorsed at Extraterrestrial Properties Agency

Surface area:	.87 Earth normal
Gravity:	.93 Earth normal
Diurnal rotation:	22.15 Earth hours
Annual revolution:	2.97 Earth years
Atmosphere:	Invigorating
Climate:	Salubrious
Noxious conditions and influences:	None
Population:	1

Mail pointed to a spot on the eastern shore of Gaea. "I live here. Just got a rough camp at present. I need money to do a bit better for myself. I'm willing to lease off one of the smaller continents, or, if you prefer, a section of Gaea, say from Murky Mountains west to the ocean."

Ullward, with a cheerful smile, shook his head. "No sections for me, Lamster Mail. I want to buy the world outright. You set your price; if it's within reason, I'll write a check."

Mail glanced at him sidewise.

"You haven't even seen the photographs."

"True." In a businesslike voice, Ullward said, "By all means, the photographs."

Mail touched the projection button. Landscapes of an unfamiliar wild beauty appeared on the screen. There were mountain crags and roaring rivers, snow-powdered forests, ocean dawns and prairie sunsets, green hillsides, meadows spattered with blossoms, beaches white as milk.

"Very pleasant," said Ullward. "Quite nice." He pulled out his checkbook. "What's your price?"

Mail chuckled and shook his head. "I won't tell. I'm willing to lease off a section—providing my price is met and my rules are agreed to."

Ullward sat with compressed lips. He gave his head a quick little jerk. Mail started to rise to his feet.

"No, no," said Ullward hastily. "I was merely thinking ... Let's look at the map again."

Mail returned the map to the screen. Ullward made careful inspection of the various continents, inquired as to physiography, climate, flora, and fauna.

Finally he made his decision. "I'll lease Gaea."

"No, Lamster Ullward!" declared Mail. "I'm reserving this entire area—from Murky Mountain and the Calliope River east. This western section is open. It's maybe a little smaller than Atalanta or Persephone, but the climate is warmer."

"There aren't any mountains on the western section," Ullward protested. "Only these insignificant Rock Castle Crags."

"They're not so insignificant," said Mail. "You've also got the Purple Bird Hills, and down here in the south is Mount Cariasco—a live volcano. What more do you need?"

88

Ullward glanced across his ranch. "I'm in the habit of thinking big."

"West Gaea is a pretty big chunk of property."

"Very well," said Ullward. "What are your terms?"

"So far as money goes, I'm not greedy," Mail said. "For a twenty-year lease: two hundred thousand a year, the first five years in advance."

Ullward made a startled protest. "Great guns, Lamster Mail! That's almost half my income!"

Mail shrugged. "I'm not trying to get rich. I want to build a lodge for myself. It costs money. If you can't afford it, I'll have to speak to someone who can."

Ullward said in a nettled voice, "I can afford it, certainly—but my entire ranch here cost less than a million."

"Well, either you want it or you don't," said Mail. "I'll tell you my rules, then you can make up your mind."

"What rules?" demanded Ullward, his face growing red.

"They're simple and their only purpose is to maintain privacy for both of us. First, you have to stay on your own property. No excursions hither and yon on my property. Second, no subleasing. Third, no residents except yourself, your family, and your servants. I don't want any artists' colony springing up, nor any wild noisy resort atmosphere. Naturally you're entitled to bring out your guests, but they've got to keep to your property just like yourself."

He looked sideways at Ullward's glum face. "I'm not trying to be tough, Lamster Ullward. Good fences make good neighbors, and it's better that we have the understanding now than hard words and beam-gun evictions later."

"Let me see the photographs again," said Ullward. "Show me West Gaea."

He looked, heaved a deep sigh. "Very well. I agree."

The construction crew had departed. Ullward was alone on West Gaea. He walked around the new lodge, taking deep breaths of pure quiet air, thrilling to the absolute solitude and privacy. The lodge had cost a fortune, but how many other people of Earth owned—leased, rather—anything to compare with this?

He walked out on the front terrace, gazed proudly across miles—genuine unsimulated miles—of landscape. For his home site, he had selected a shelf in the foothills of the Ullward Range (as he had renamed the Purple Bird Hills). In front spread a great golden savannah dotted with blue-green trees; behind rose a tall gray cliff.

A stream rushed down a cleft in the rock, leaping, splashing, cooling the air, finally flowing into a beautiful clear pool, beside which Ullward had erected a cabana of red, green and brown plastic. At the base of the cliff and in crevices grew clumps of spiky blue cactus, lush green bushes covered with red trumpet-flowers, a thick-leafed white plant holding up a stalk clustered with white bubbles.

Solitude! The real thing! No thumping of factories, no roar of traffic two feet from one's bed. One arm outstretched, the other pressed to his chest, Ullward performed a stately little jig of triumph on the terrace. Had he been able, he might have turned a cartwheel. When a person has complete privacy, absolutely nothing is forbidden!

Ullward took a final turn up and down the terrace, made a last appreciative survey of the horizon. The sun was sinking through banks of fire-fringed clouds. Marvelous depth of color, a tonal brilliance to be matched only in the very best illusion-panes!

He entered the lodge, made a selection from the nutrition locker. After a leisurely meal, he returned to the lounge. He stood thinking for a moment, then went out upon the terrace, strolled up and down. Wonderful! The night was full of stars, hanging like blurred white lamps, almost as he had always imagined them.

After ten minutes of admiring the stars, he returned into the lodge. Now what? The wall-screen, with its assortment of recorded programs. Snug and comfortable, Ullward watched the performance of a recent musical comedy.

Real luxury, he told himself. Pity he couldn't invite his

friends out to spend the evening. Unfortunately impossible, considering the inconvenient duration of the trip between Mail's Planet and Earth. However—only three days until the arrival of his first guest. She was Elf Intry, a young woman who had been more than friendly with Ullward on Earth. When Elf arrived, Ullward would broach a subject which he had been mulling over for several months—indeed, ever since he had first learned of Mail's Planet.

Elf Intry arrived early in the afternoon, coming down to Mail's Planet in a capsule discharged from the weekly Outer Ring Express packet. A woman of normally good disposition, she greeted Ullward in a seethe of indignation. "Just who is that brute around the other side of the planet? I thought you had absolute privacy here!"

"That's just old Mail," said Ullward evasively. "What's wrong?"

"The fool on the packet set me the wrong coordinates and the capsule came down on a beach. I noticed a house and then I saw a naked man jumping rope behind some bushes. I thought it was you, of course. I went over and said 'Boo!' You should have *heard* the language he used!" She shook her head. "I don't see why you allow such a boor on your planet."

The buzzer on the communication screen sounded. "That's Mail now," said Ullward. "You wait here. I'll tell him how to speak to *my* guests!"

He presently returned to the terrace. Elf came over to him, kissed his nose. "Ully, you're pale with rage! I hope you didn't lose your temper."

"No," said Ullward. "We merely—well, we had an understanding. Come along, look over the property."

He took Elf around to the back, pointing out the swimming pool, the waterfall, the mass of rock above. "You won't see that effect on any illusion-pane! That's genuine rock!"

"Lovely, Ully. Very nice. The color might be just a trifle darker, though. Rock doesn't look like that."

"No?" Ullward inspected the cliff more critically.

"Well, I can't do anything about it. How about the privacy?"

"Wonderful! It's so quiet, it's almost eerie!"

"Eerie?" Ullward looked around the landscape. "It hadn't occurred to me."

"You're not sensitive to these things, Ully. Still, it's very nice, if you can tolerate that unpleasant creature Mail so close."

"Close?" protested Ullward. "He's on the other side of the continent!"

"True," said Elf. "It's all relative, I suppose. How long do you expect to stay out here?"

"That depends. Come along inside. I want to talk with you."

He seated her in a comfortable chair, brought her a globe of Gluco-Fructoid Nectar. For himself, he mixed ethyl alcohol, water, a few drops of Haig's Oldtime Esters.

"Elf, where do you stand in the reproduction list?"

She raised her fine eyebrows, shook her head. "So far down, I've lost count. Fifty or sixty billion."

"I'm down thirty-seven billion. It's one reason I bought this place. Waiting list, piffle! Nobody stops Bruham Ullward's breeding on his own planet!"

Elf pursed her lips, shook her head sadly. "It won't work, Ully."

"And why not?"

"You can't take the children back to Earth. The list would keep them out."

"True, but think of living here, surrounded by children. All the children you wanted! And utter privacy to boot! What more could you ask for?"

Elf sighed. "You fabricate a beautiful illusion-pane, Ully. But I think not. I love the privacy and solitude—but I thought there'd be more people to be private from."

The Outer Ring Express packet came past four days later. Elf kissed Ullward good-bye. "It's simply exquisite here, Ully. The solitude is so magnificent, it gives me gooseflesh. I've had a wonderful visit." She climbed into the capsule. "See you on Earth."

"Just a minute," said Ullward suddenly. "I want you to post a letter or two for me."

"Hurry. I've only got twenty minutes."

Ullward was back in ten minutes. "Invitations," he told her breathlessly. "Friends."

"Right." She kissed his nose. "Good-bye, Ully." She slammed the port; the capsule rushed away, whirling up to meet the packet.

The new guests arrived three weeks later: Frobisher Worbeck, Liornetta Stobart, Harris and Hyla Cabe, Ted and Ravelin and Iugenae Seehoe, Juvenal Aquister and his son, Runy.

Ullward, brown from long days of lazing in the sun, greeted them with great enthusiasm. "Welcome to my little retreat! Wonderful to see you all! Frobisher, you pink-cheeked rascal! And Iugenae! Prettier than ever! Be careful, Ravelin—I've got my eye on your daughter! But Runy's here, guess I'm out of the picture! Liornetta, damned glad you could make it! And Ted! Great to see you, old chap! This is all your doing, you know! Harris, Hyla, Juvenal—come on up! We'll have a drink, a drink, a drink!"

Running from one to the other, patting arms, herding the slow-moving Frobisher Worbeck, he conducted his guests up the slope to the terrace. Here they turned to survey the panorama. Ullward listened to their remarks, mouth pursed against a grin of gratification.

"Magnificent!"

"Grand!"

"Absolutely genuine!"

"The sky is so far away, it frightens me!"

"The sunlight's so pure!"

"The genuine thing's always best, isn't it?"

Runy said a trifle wistfully, "I thought you were on a beach, Lamster Ullward."

"Beach? This is mountain country, Runy. Land of the wide open spaces! Look out over that plain!"

Liornetta Stobart patted Runy's shoulder. "Not every planet has beaches, Runy. The secret of happiness is to be content with what one has."

93

Ullward laughed gaily. "Oh, I've got beaches, never fear for that! There's a fine beach—ha, ha—five hundred miles due west. Every step Ullward domain!"

"Can we go?" asked Iugenae excitedly. "Can we go, Lamster Ullward?"

"We certainly can! That shed down the slope is headquarters for the Ullward Airlines. We'll fly to the beach, swim in Ullward Ocean! But now refreshment! After that crowded capsule, your throats must be like paper!"

"It wasn't too crowded," said Ravelin Seehoe. "There were only nine of us." She looked critically up at the cliff. "If that were an illusion-pane, I'd consider it grotesque."

"My dear Ravelin!" cried Ullward. "It's impressive! Magnificent!"

"All of that," agreed Frobisher Worbeck, a tall, sturdy man, white-haired, red-jowled, with a blue benevolent gaze. "And now, Bruham, what about those drinks?"

"Of course! Ted, I know you of old. Will you tend bar? Here's the alcohol, here's water, here are the esters. Now, you two," Ullward called to Runy and Iugenae. "How about some nice cold soda pop?"

"What kind is there?" asked Runy.

"All kinds, all flavors. This is Ullward's Retreat! We've got methylamyl glutamine, cycloprodacterol phosphate, metathiobromine-4-glycocitrose . . ."

Runy and Iugenae expressed their preferences; Ullward brought the globes, then hurried to arrange tables and chairs for the adults. Presently everyone was comfortable and relaxed.

Iugenae whispered to Ravelin, who smiled and nodded indulgently. "Lamster Ullward, you remember the beautiful oak leaf you gave Iugenae?"

"Of course I do."

"It's still as fresh and green as ever. I wonder if Iugenae might have a leaf or two from some of these other trees?"

"My dear Ravelin!" Ullward roared with laughter. "She can have an entire tree!"

"Oh, Mother! Can—"

"Iugenae, don't be ridiculous!" snapped Ted. "How

could we get it home? Where would we plant the thing? In the bathroom?"

Ravelin said, "You and Runy find some nice leaves, but don't wander too far."

"No, Mother." She beckoned to Runy. "Come along, dope. Bring a basket."

The others of the party gazed out over the plain. "A beautiful view, Ullward," said Frobisher Worbeck. "How far does your property extend?"

"Five hundred miles west to the ocean, six hundred miles east to the mountains, eleven hundred miles north and two hundred miles south."

Worbeck shook his head solemnly. "Nice. A pity you couldn't get the whole planet. Then you'd have real privacy!"

"I tried, of course," said Ullward. "The owner refused to consider the idea."

"A pity."

Ullward brought out a map. "However, as you see, I have a fine volcano, a number of excellent rivers, a mountain range, and down here on the delta of Cinnamon River an absolutely miasmic swamp."

Ravelin pointed to the ocean. "Why, it's Lonesome Ocean! I thought the name was Ullward Ocean."

Ullward laughed uncomfortably. "Just a figure of speech—so to speak. My rights extend ten miles. More than enough for swimming purposes."

"No freedom of the seas here, eh, Lamster Ullward?" laughed Harris Cabe.

"Not exactly," confessed Ullward.

"A pity," said Frobisher Worbeck.

Hyla Cabe pointed to the map. "Look at these wonderful mountain ranges! The Magnificent Mountains! And over here—the Elysian Gardens! I'd love to see them, Lamster Ullward."

Ullward shook his head in embarrassment. "Impossible, I'm afraid. They're not on my property. I haven't even seen them myself."

His guests stared at him in astonishment. "But surely—"

"It's an atom-welded contract with Lamster Mail," Ullward explained. "He stays on his property, I stay on mine. In this way, our privacy is secure."

"Look," Hyla Cabe said aside to Ravelin, "the Unimaginable Caverns! Doesn't it make you simply wild not to be able to see them?"

Aquister said hurriedly, "It's a pleasure to sit here and just breathe this wonderful fresh air. No noise, no crowds, no bustle or hurry."

The party drank and chatted and basked in the sunshine until late afternoon. Enlisting the aid of Ravelin Seehoe and Hyla Cabe, Ullward set out a simple meal of yeast pellets, processed protein, thick slices of algae crunch.

"No animal flesh, cooked vegetation?" questioned Worbeck curiously.

"Tried them the first day," said Ullward. "Revolting. Sick for a week."

After dinner, the guests watched a comic melodrama on the wallscreen. Then Ullward showed them to their various cubicles, and after a few minutes of badinage and calling back and forth, the lodge became quiet.

Next day, Ullward ordered his guests into their bathing suits. "We're off to the beach, we'll gambol on the sand, we'll frolic in the surf of Lonesome Ullward Ocean!"

The guests piled happily into the air-car. Ullward counted heads. "All aboard! We're off!"

They rose and flew west, first low over the plain, then high into the air, to obtain a panoramic view of the Rock Castle Crags.

"The tallest peak—there to the north—is almost ten thousand feet high. Notice how it juts up, just imagine the mass! Solid rock! How'd you like that dropped on your toe, Runy? No so good, eh? In a moment, we'll see a precipice over a thousand feet straight up and down. There—now! Isn't that remarkable?"

"Certainly impressive," agreed Ted.

"What those Magnificent Mountains must be like!" said Harris Cabe with a wry laugh.

"How tall are they, Lamster Ullward?" inquired Liornetta Stobart.

"What? Which?"

"The Magnificent Mountains."

"I don't know for sure. Thirty or forty thousand feet, I suppose."

"What a marvelous sight they must be!" Said Frobisher Worbeck. "Probably make these look like foothills."

"These are beautiful too," Hyla Cabe put in hastily.

"Oh, naturally," said Frobisher Worbeck. "A damned fine sight! You're a lucky man, Bruham!"

Ullward laughed shortly, turned the air-car west. They flew across a rolling forested plain and presently Lonesome Ocean gleamed in the distance. Ullward slanted down, landed the air-car on the beach, and the party alighted.

The day was warm, the sun hot. A fresh wind blew in from the ocean. The surf broke upon the sand in massive roaring billows.

The party stood appraising the scene. Ullward swung his arms. "Well, who's for it? Don't wait to be invited! We've got the whole ocean to ourselves!"

Ravelin said, "It's so rough! Look how that water crashes down!"

Liornetta Stobart turned away with a shake of her head. "Illusion-pane surf is always so gentle. This could lift you right up and give you a good shaking!"

"I expected nothing quite so vehement," Harris Cabe admitted.

Ravelin beckoned to Iugenae. "You keep well away, Miss Puss. I don't want you swept out to sea. You'd find it Lonesome Ocean indeed!"

Runy approached the water, waded gingerly into a sheet of retreating foam. A comber thrashed down at him and he danced quickly back to the shore.

"The water's cold," he reported.

Ullward poised himself. "Well, here goes! I'll show you how it's done!" He trotted forward, stopped short, then flung himself into the face of a great white comber.

The party on the beach watched.

"Where is he?" asked Hyla Cabe.

97

Iugenae pointed. "I saw part of him out there. A leg, or an arm."

"There he is!" cried Ted. "Woof! Another one's caught him. I suppose some people might consider it sport . . ."

Ullward staggered to his feet, lurched through the retreating wash to shore. "Hah! Great! Invigorating! Ted! Harris! Juvenal! Take a go at it!"

Harris shook his head. "I don't think I'll try it today, Bruham."

"The next time for me too," said Juvenal Aquister. "Perhaps it won't be so rough."

"But don't let us stop you!" urged Ted. "You swim as long as you like. We'll wait here for you."

"Oh, I've had enough for now," said Ullward. "Excuse me while I change."

When Ullward returned, he found his guests seated in the air-car. "Hello! Everyone ready to go?"

"It's hot in the sun," explained Liornetta, "and we thought we'd enjoy the view better from inside."

"When you look through the glass, it's almost like an illusion-pane," said Iugenae.

"Oh, I see. Well, perhaps you're ready to visit other parts of the Ullward domain?"

The proposal met with approval; Ullward took the air-car into the air. "We can fly north over the pine woods, south over Mount Cairasco, which unfortunately isn't erupting just now."

"Anywhere you like, Lamster Ullward," said Frobisher Worbeck. "No doubt it's all beautiful."

Ullward considered the varied attractions of his leasehold. "Well, first to the Cinnamon Swamp."

For two hours they flew, over the swamp, across the smoking crater of Mount Cairasco, east to the edge of Murky Mountains, along Calliope River to its source in Goldenleaf Lake. Ullward pointed out noteworthy views, interesting aspects. Behind him, the murmurs of admiration dwindled and finally died.

"Had enough?" Ullward called back gaily. "Can't see half a continent in one day! Shall we save some for tomorrow?"

There was a moment's stillness. Then Liornetta Stobart

said, "Lamster Ullward, we're simply dying for a peek at the Magnificent Mountains. I wonder—do you think we could slip over for a quick look? I'm sure Lamster Mail wouldn't really mind."

Ullward shook his head with a rather stiff smile. "He's made me agree to a very definite set of rules. I've already had one brush with him."

"How could he possibly find out?" asked Juvenal Aquister.

"He probably wouldn't find out," said Ullward, "but—"

"It's a damned shame for him to lock you off into this drab little peninsula!" Frobisher Worbeck said indignantly.

"Please, Lamster Ullward," Iugenae wheedled.

"Oh, very well," Ullward said recklessly.

He turned the air-car east. The Murky Mountains passed below. The party peered from the windows, exclaiming at the marvels of the forbidden landscape.

"How far are the Magnificent Mountains?" asked Ted.

"Not far. Another thousand miles."

"Why are you hugging the ground?" asked Frobisher Worbeck. "Up in the air, man! Let's see the countryside!"

Ullward hesitated. Mail was probably asleep. And, in the last analysis, he really had no right to forbid an innocent little—

"Lamster Ullward," called Runy, "there's an air-car right behind us."

The air-car drew up level. Kennes Mail's blue eyes met Ullward's across the gap. He motioned Ullward down.

Ullward compressed his mouth, swung the air-car down. From behind him came murmurs of symptahy and outrage.

Below was a dark pine forest; Ullward set down in a pretty little glade. Mail landed nearby, jumped to the ground, signaled to Ullward. The two men walked to the side. The guests murmured together and shook their heads.

Ullward presently returned to the air-car. "Everybody please get in," he said crisply.

They rose into the air and flew west. "What did the chap have to say for himself?" queried Worbeck.

Ullward chewed at his lips. "Not too much. Wanted to know if I'd lost the way. I told him one or two things. Reached an understanding . . ." His voice dwindled, then rose in a burst of cheerfulness. "We'll have a party back at the lodge. What do we care for Mail and his confounded mountains?"

"That's the spirit, Bruham!" cried Frobisher Worbeck.

Both Ted and Ullward tended bar during the evening. Either one or the other mingled rather more alcohol to rather less esters into the drinks than standard practice recommended. As a result, the party became quite loud and gay. Ullward damned Mail's interfering habits; Worbeck explored six thousand years of common law in an effort to prove Mail a domineering tyrant; the women giggled; Iugenae and Runy watched cynically, then presently went off to attend to their own affairs.

In the morning, the group slept late. Ullward finally tottered out on the terrace, to be joined one at a time by the others. Runy and Iugenae were missing.

"Young rascals," groaned Worbeck. "If they're lost, they'll have to find their own way back. No search parties for me."

At noon, Runy and Iugenae returned in Ullward's air-car.

"Good heavens," shrieked Ravelin. "Iugenae, come here this instant! Where have you been?"

Juvenal Aquister surveyed Runy sternly. "Have you lost your mind, taking Lamster Ullward's air-car without his permission?"

"I asked him last night," Runy declared indignantly. "He said yes, take anything except the volcano because that's where he slept when his feet got cold, and the swamp because that's where he dropped his empty containers."

"Regardless," said Juvenal in disgust, "you should have had better sense. Where have you been?"

Runy fidgeted. Iugenae said, "Well, we went south for a while, then turned and went east—I think it was east. We thought if we flew low, Lamster Mail wouldn't see us. So we flew low, through the mountains, and pretty soon

100

we came to an ocean. We went along the beach and came to a house. We landed to see who lived there, but nobody was home."

Ullward stiffled a groan.

"What would anyone want with a pen of birds?" asked Runy.

"Birds? What birds? Where?"

"At the house. There was a pen with a lot of big birds, but they kind of got loose while we were looking at them and all flew away."

"Anyway," Iugenae continued briskly, "we decided it was Lamster Mail's house, so we wrote a note, telling what everybody thinks of him and pinned it to his door."

Ullward rubbed his forehead. "Is that all?"

"Well, practically all." Iugenae became diffident. She looked at Runy and the two of them giggled nervously.

"There's more?" yelled Ullward. "What, in heaven's name?"

"Nothing very much," said Iugenae, following a crack in the terrace with her toe. "We put a booby-trap over the door—just a bucket of water. Then we came home."

The screen buzzer sounded from inside the lodge. Everybody looked at Ullward. Ullward heaved a deep sigh, rose to his feet, went inside.

That very afternoon, the Outer Ring Express packet was due to pass the junction point. Frobisher Worbeck felt sudden and acute qualms of conscience for the neglect his business suffered while he dawdled away hours in idle enjoyment.

"But my dear old chap!" exclaimed Ullward. "Relaxation is good for you!"

True, agreed Frobisher Worbeck, if one could make himself oblivious to the possibility of fiasco through the carelessness of underlings. Much as he deplored the necessity, in spite of his inclination to loiter for weeks, he felt impelled to leave—and not a minute later than that very afternoon.

Others of the group likewise remembered important business which they had to see to, and those remaining felt it would be a shame and an imposition to send up the capsule half-empty and likewise decided to return.

Ullward's arguments met unyielding walls of obstinacy. Rather glumly, he went down to the capsule to bid his guests farewell. As they climbed through the port, they expressed their parting thanks:

"Bruham, it's been absolutely marvelous!"

"You'll never know how we've enjoyed this outing, Lamster Ullward!"

"The air, the space, the privacy—I'll never forget!"

"It was the most, to say the least."

The port thumped into its socket. Ullward stood back, waving rather uncertainly.

Ted Seehoe reached to press the Active button. Ullward sprang forward, pounded on the port.

"Wait!" he bellowed. "A few things I've got to attend to! I'm coming with you!"

"Come in, come in," said Ullward heartily, opening the door to three of his friends: Coble and his wife, Heulia Sansom, and Coble's young, pretty cousin Landine. "Glad to see you!"

"And we're glad to come! We've heard so much of your wonderful ranch, we've been on pins and needles all day!"

"Oh, come now! It's not so marvelous as all that!"

"Not to you, perhaps—you live here!"

Ullward smiled. "Well, I must say I live here and still like it. Would you like to have lunch, or perhaps you'd prefer to walk around for a few minutes? I've just finished making a few changes, but I'm happy to say everything is in order."

"Can we just take a look?"

"Of course. Come over here. Stand just so. Now—are you ready?"

"Ready."

Ullward snapped the wall back.

"Ooh!" breathed Landine. "Isn't it beautiful!"

"The space, the open feeling!"

"Look, a tree! What a wonderful simulation!"

102

"That's no simulation," said Ullward. "That's a genuine tree!"

"Lamster Ullward, are you telling the truth?"

"I certainly am. I never tell lies to a lovely young lady. Come along, over this way."

"Lamster Ullward, that cliff is so convincing, it frightens me."

Ullward grinned. "It's a good job." He signaled a halt. "Now—turn around."

The group turned. They looked out across a great golden savannah, dotted with groves of blue-green trees. A rustic lodge commanded the view, the door being the opening into Ullward's living room.

The group stood in silent admiration. Then Heulia sighed. "Space. Pure space."

"I'd swear I was looking miles," said Coble.

Ullward smiled, a trifle wistfully. "Glad you like my little retreat. Now what about lunch? Genuine algae!"

THE GIFT OF GAB

Middle afternoon had come to the Shallows; the wind had died, the sea was listless and spread with silken gloss. In the south a black broom of rain hung under the clouds; elsewhere the air was thick with pink murk. Thick crusts of seaweed floated over the Shallows; one of these supported the Bio-Minerals raft, a metal rectangle two hundred feet long, a hundred feet wide.

At four o'clock an air horn high on the mast announced the change of shift. Sam Fletcher, assistant superintendent, came out of the mess hall, crossed the deck to the office, slid back the door, looked in. Where Carl Raight usually sat, filing out his production report, the chair was empty. Fletcher looked over his shoulder, down the deck toward the processing house, but Raight was nowhere in sight. Strange. Fletcher crossed the office, checked the day's tonnage:

Rhodium trichloride 4.01
Tantalum sulfide 0.87
Tripyridyl rhenichloride 0.43

The gross tonnage, by Fletcher's calculations, came to 5.31—an average shift. He still led Raight in the Pinch-bottle Sweepstakes. Tomorrow was the end of the month; Fletcher could hardly fail to make off with Raight's Haig & Haig. Anticipating Right's protests and complaints, Fletcher smiled and whistled through his teeth. He felt cheerful and confident. Another month would bring to an end his six-months contract; then it was back to Star-holme with six months' pay to his credit.

Where in thunder was Raight? Fletcher looked out the window. In his range of vision was the helicopter—guyed to the deck against the Sabrian line-squalls—the mast, the black hump of the generator, the water tank, and at the far end of the raft, the pulverizers, the leaching vats, the Tswett columns, and the storage bins.

A dark shape filled the door. Fletcher turned, but it was Agostino, the day-shift operator, who had just now been relieved by Blue Murphy, Fletcher's operator.

"Where's Raight?" asked Fletcher.

Agostino looked around the office.

"I thought he was in here."

"I thought he was over in the works."

"No, I just came from there."

Fletcher crossed the room, looked into the washroom. "Wrong again."

Agostino turned away. "I'm going up for a shower." He looked back from the door. "We're low on barnacles."

"I'll send out the barge." Fletcher followed Agostino out on deck, headed for the processing house.

He passed the dock where the barges were tied up, entered the pulverizing room. The No. 1 Rotary was grinding barnacles for tantalum; the No. 2 was pulverizing rhenium-rich sea slugs. The ball mill waited for a load of coral, orange-pink with nodules of rhodium salts.

Blue Murphy, who had a red face and a meager fringe of red hair, was making a routine check of bearings, shafts, chains, journals, valves, and gauges. Fletcher called in his ear to be heard over the noise of the crushers, "Has Raight come through?"

Murphy shook his head.

Fletcher went on, into the leaching chamber where the first separation of salts from pulp was effected, through the forest of Tswett tubes, and once more out upon the deck. No Raight. He must have gone on ahead to the office.

But the office was empty.

Fletcher continued around to the mess hall. Agostino was busy with a bowl of chili. Dave Jones, the hatchet-faced steward, stood in the doorway to the galley.

"Raight been here?" asked Fletcher.

Jones, who never used two words when one would do,

105

gave his head a morose shake. Agostino looked around. "Did you check the barnacle barge? He might have gone out to the shelves."

Fletcher looked puzzled. "What's wrong with Mahlberg?"

"He's putting new teeth on the drag-line bucket."

Fletcher tried to recall the lineup of barges along the dock. If Mahlberg, the barge tender, had been busy with repairs, Raight might well have gone out himself. Fletcher drew himself a cup of coffee. "That's where he must be." He sat down. "It's not like Raight to put in free overtime."

Mahlberg came into the mess hall. "Where's Carl? I want to order some more teeth for the bucket."

"He's gone fishing," said Agostino.

Mahlberg laughed at the joke. "Catch himself a nice wire eel maybe. Or a dekabrach."

Dave Jones grunted. "He'll cook it himself."

"Seems like a dekabrach should make good eatin'," said Mahlberg, "close as they are to a seal."

"Who likes seal?" growled Jones.

"I'd say they're more like mermaids," Agostino remarked, "with ten-armed starfish for heads."

Fletcher put down his cup. "I wonder what time Raight left?"

Mahlberg shrugged; Agostino looked blank.

"It's only an hour out to the shelves. He ought to be back by now."

"He might have had a breakdown," said Mahlberg. "Although the barge has been running good."

Fletcher rose to his feet. "I'll give him a call." He left the mess hall, returned to the office, where he dialed T3 on the intercom screen—the signal for the barnacle barge.

The screen remained blank.

Fletcher waited. The neon bulb pulsed off and on, indicating the call of the alarm on the barge.

No reply.

Fletcher felt a vague disturbance. He left the office, went to the mast, rode up the man-list to the cupola. From here he could overlook the half-acre of raft, the five-acre crust of seaweed, and a great circle of ocean.

In the far northeast distance, up near the edge of the Shallows, the new Pelagic Recoveries raft showed as a small dark spot, almost smeared from sight by the haze. To the south, where the Equatorial Current raced through a gap in the Shallows, the barnacle shelves were strung out in a long loose line. To the north, where the Macpherson Ridge, rising from the Deeps, came within thirty feet of breaking the surface, aluminum piles supported the sea-slug traps. Here and there floated masses of seaweed, sometimes anchored to the bottom, sometimes maintained in place by action of the currents.

Fletcher turned binoculars along the line of barnacle shelves, spotted the barge immediately. He steadied his arms, screwed up the magnification, focused on the control cabin. He saw no one, although he could not hold the binoculars steady enough to make sure.

Fletcher scrutinized the rest of the barge.

Where was Carl Raight? Possibly in the control cabin, out of sight.

Fletcher descended to the deck, went around to the processing house, looked in. "Hey, Blue!"

Murphy appeared, wiping his big red hands on a rag.

"I'm taking the launch out to the shelves," said Fletcher. "The barge is out there, but Raight doesn't answer the screen."

Murphy shook his big bald head in puzzlement. He accompanied Fletcher to the dock, where the launch floated at moorings. Fletcher heaved at the painter, swung in the stern of the launch, jumped down on the deck.

Murphy called down to him, "Want me to come along? I'll get Hans to watch the works." Hans Heinz was the engineer-mechanic.

Fletcher hesitated. "I don't think so. If anything's happened to Raight—well, I can manage. Just keep an eye on the screen. I might call back in."

He stepped into the cockpit, seated himself, closed the dome over his head, started the pump.

The launch rolled and bounced, picked up speed, shoved its blunt nose under the surface, submerged till only the dome was clear.

Fletcher disengaged the pump; water rammed in through the nose, converted to steam, spat aft.

Bio-Minerals became a gray blot in the pink haze, while the outlines of the barge and the shelves became hard and distinct and gradually grew large. Fletcher de-staged the power; the launch surfaced, coasted up to the dark hull, grappled with magnetic balls that allowed barge and launch to surge independently on the slow swells.

Fletcher slid back the dome, jumped up to the deck.

"Raight! Hey, Carl!"

There was no answer.

Fletcher looked up and down the deck. Raight was a big man, strong and active—but there might have been an accident. Fletcher walked down the deck toward the control cabin. He passed the No. 1 hold, heaped with black-green barnacles. At the No. 2 hold the boom was winged out, with the grab engaged on a shelf, ready to hoist it clear of the water.

The No. 3 hold was still unladen. The control cabin was empty.

Carl Raight was nowhere aboard the barge.

He might have been taken off by helicopter or launch, or he might have fallen over the side. Fletcher made a slow check of the dark water in all directions. He suddenly leaned over the side, trying to see through the surface reflections. But the pale shape under the water was a dekabrach, long as a man, sleek as satin, moving quietly about its business.

Fletcher looked thoughtfully to the northeast, where the Pelagic Recoveries raft floated behind a curtain of pink murk. It was a new venture, only three months old, owned and operated by Ted Chrystal, former biochemist on the Bio-Minerals raft. The Sabrian Ocean was inexhaustible; the market for metal was insatiable; the two rafts were in no sense competitors. By no stretch of imagination could Fletcher conceive Chrystal or his men attacking Carl Raight.

He must have fallen overboard.

Fletcher returned to the control cabin, climbed the ladder to the flying bridge on top. He made a last check of the water around the barge, although he knew it to be a useless gesture—the current, moving through the gap at a steady two knots, would have swept Raight's body out over the Deeps. Fletcher scanned the horizon. The line of shelves dwindled away into the pink gloom. The mast on the Bio-Minerals raft marked the sky to the northwest. The Pelagic Recoveries raft could not be seen. There was no living creature in sight.

The screen signal sounded from the cabin. Fletcher went inside. Blue Murphy was calling from the raft. "What's the news?"

"None whatever," said Fletcher.

"What do you mean?"

"Raight's not out here."

The big red face creased. "Just who is out there?"

"Nobody. It looks like Raight fell over the side."

Murphy whistled. There seemed nothing to say. Finally he asked, "Any idea how it happened?"

Fletcher shook his head. "I can't figure it out."

Murphy licked his lips. "Maybe we ought to close down."

"Why?" asked Fletcher.

"Well—reverence to the dead, you might say."

Fletcher grinned crookedly. "We might as well keep running."

"Just as you like. But we're low on the barnacles."

"Carl loaded a hold and a half—" Fletcher hesitated, heaved a deep sigh. "I might as well shake in a few more shelves."

Murphy winced. "It's a squeamish business, Sam. You haven't a nerve in your body."

"It doesn't make any difference to Carl now," said Fletcher. "We've got to scrape barnacles sometime. There's nothing to be gained by moping."

"I suppose you're right," said Murphy dubiously.

"I'll be back in a couple hours."

"Don't go overboard like Raight, now."

The screen went blank. Fletcher reflected that he was in charge, superintendent of the raft, until the arrival of the new crew, a month away. Responsibility, which he did not particularly want, was his.

He went slowly back out on deck, climbed into the winch pulpit. For an hour he pulled sections of shelves from the sea, suspended them over the hold while scraper arms wiped off the black-green clusters, then slid the shelves back into the ocean. Here was where Raight had been working just before his disappearance. How could he have fallen overboard from the winch pulpit?

Uneasiness inched along Fletcher's nerves, up into his brain. He shut down the winch, climbed down from the pulpit. He stopped short, staring at the rope on the deck.

It was a strange rope—glistening, translucent, an inch thick. It lay in a loose loop on the deck and one end led over the side. Feltcher started down, then hesitated. Rope? Certainly none of the barge's equipment.

Careful, thought Fletcher.

A hand-scraper hung on the king-post, a tool like a small adze. It was used for manual scraping of the shelves, if for some reason the automatic scrapers failed. It was two steps distant, across the rope. Fletcher stepped down to the deck. The rope quivered; the loop contracted, snapped around Fletcher's ankles.

Fletcher lunged, caught hold of the scraper. The rope gave a cruel jerk; Fletcher sprawled flat on his face and the scraper jarred out of his hands. He kicked, struggled, but the rope drew him easily toward the gunwale. Fletcher made a convulsive grab for the scraper, barely reached it. The rope was lifting his ankles, to pull him over the rail. Fletcher strained forward, hacked, again and again. The rope sagged, fell apart, snaked over the side.

Fletcher gained his feet, staggered to the rail. Down into the water slid the rope, out of sight among the oily reflections of the sky. Then, for half a second, a wave-front held itself perpendicular to Fletcher's line of vision. Three feet under the surface swam a dekabrach. Fletcher saw the pink-golden cluster of arms, radiating like the arms of a starfish, the black patch at their core which might be an eye.

Fletcher drew back from the gunwale, puzzled, frightened, oppressed by the nearness of death. He cursed his stupidity, his reckless carelessness; how could he have been so undiscerning as to remain out here loading the

110

barge? It was clear from the first that Raight had never died by accident. Something had killed Raight, and Fletcher had invited it to kill him too. He limped to the control cabin, started the pumps. Water sucked in through the bow orifice, thrust out through the vents. The barge moved out away from the shelves; Fletcher set the course to northwest, toward Bio-Minerals, then went out on deck.

Day was almost at an end; the sky was darkening to maroon; the gloom grew thick as bloody water. Geidion, a dull red giant, largest of Sabria's two suns, dropped out of the sky. For a few minutes only the light from blue-green Atreus played on the clouds. The gloom changed its quality to pale green, which by some illusion seemed brighter than the previous pink. Atreus sank and the sky went dark.

Ahead shone the Bio-Minerals masthead light, climbing into the sky as the barge approached. Fletcher saw the black shapes of men outlined against the glow. The entire crew was waiting for him: the two operators, Agostino and Murphy, Mahlberg the barge tender, Damon the biochemist, Dave Jones the steward, Manners the technician, Hans Heinz the engineer.

Fletcher docked the barge, climbed the soft stairs hacked from the wadded seaweed, stopped in front of the silent men. He looked from face to face. Waiting on the raft they had felt the strangeness of Raight's death more vividly than he had; so much showed in their expressions.

Fletcher, answering the unspoken question, said, "It wasn't an accident. I know what happened."

"What?" someone asked.

"There's a thing like a white rope," said Fletcher. "It slides up out of the sea. If a man comes near it, it snaps around his leg and pulls him overboard."

Murphy asked in a hushed voice, "You're sure?"

"It just about got me."

Damon the biochemist asked in a skeptical voice, "A live rope?"

"I suppose it might have been alive."

"What else could it have been?"

Fletcher hesitated. "I looked over the side. I saw deka-brachs. One for sure, maybe two or three others."

111

There was silence. The men looked out over the water. Murphy asked in a wondering voice, "Then the deka-brachs are the ones?"

"I don't know," said Fletcher in a strained, sharp voice. "A white rope, or fiber, nearly snared me. I cut it apart. When I looked over the side I saw dekabrachs."

The men made hushed noises of wonder and awe.

Fletcher turned away, started toward the mess hall. The men lingered on the dock, examining the ocean, talking in subdued voices. The lights of the raft shone past them, out into the darkness. There was nothing to be seen.

Later in the evening Fletcher climbed the stairs to the laboratory over the office, to find Eugene Damon busy at the microfilm viewer.

Damon had a thin, long-jawed face, lank blond hair, a fanatic's eyes. He was industrious and thorough, but he worked in the shadow of Ted Chrystal, who had quit Bio-Minerals to bring his own raft to Sabria. Chrystal was a man of great ability. He had adapted the vanadium-sequestering sea slug of Earth to Sabrian waters; he had developed the tantalum barnacle from a rare and sickly species into the hardy high-yield producer that it was. Damon worked twice the hours that Chrystal had put in, and while he performed his routine duties efficently, he lacked the flair and imaginative resource which Chrystal used to leap from problem to solution without apparent steps in between.

He looked up when Fletcher came into the lab, then applied himself once more to the microscreen.

Fletcher watched a moment. "What are you looking for?" he asked presently.

Damon responded in the ponderous, slightly pedantic manner that sometimes amused, sometimes irritated Fletcher. "I've been searching the index to identify the long white 'rope' which attacked you."

Fletcher made a noncommittal sound, went to look at the settings on the microfile throw-out. Damon had coded for "long," "thin," dimension classification "E, F, G." On these instructions, the selector, scanning the entire roster of Sabrian life forms, had pulled the cards of seven organisms.

112

"Find anything?" Fletcher asked.

"Not so far." Damon slid another card into the viewer. "Sabrian Annelid, RRS-4924," read the title, and on the screen appeared a schematic outline of a long segmented worm. The scale showed it to be about two and a half meters long.

Fletcher shook his head. "The thing that got me was four or five times that long. And I don't think it was segmented."

"That's the most likely of the lot so far," said Damon. He turned a quizzical glance up at Fletcher. "I imagine you're pretty sure about this . . . long white marine 'rope'?"

Fletcher ignored him, scooped up the seven cards, dropped them back into the file, looked in the code book, reset the selector.

Damon had the codes memorized and was able to read directly off the dials. " 'Appendages—'long'—'dimensions D, E, F, G'."

The selector kicked three cards into the viewer.

The first was a pale saucer which swam like a skate, trailing four long whiskers. "That's not it," said Fletcher.

The second was a black bullet-shaped water-beetle, with a posterior flagellum.

"Not that one."

The third was a kind of mollusk, with a plasm based on selenium, silicon, flourine, and carbon. The shell was a hemisphere of silicon carbide, with a hump from which protruded a thin prehensile tendril.

The creature bore the name "Stryzkal's Monitor," after Esteban Stryzkal, the famous pioneer taxonomist of Sabria.

"That might be the guilty party," said Fletcher.

"It's not mobile," objected Damon. "Stryzkal finds it anchored to the North Shallows pegmatite dikes, in conjunction with the dekabrach colonies."

Fletcher was reading the descriptive material. " 'The feeler is elastic without observable limit, and apparently functions as a food-gathering, spore-disseminating, exploratory organ. The monitor typically is found near the dekabrach colonies. Symbiosis between the two life forms is not impossible.' "

113

Damon looked at him questioningly. "Well?"

"I saw some dekabrachs out along the shelves."

"You can't be sure you were attacked by a monitor," Damon said dubiously. "After all, they don't swim."

"So they don't," said Fletcher, "according to Stryzkal."

Damon started to speak, then noticing Fletcher's expression, said in a subdued voice, "Of course, there's room for error. Not even Stryzkal could work out much more than a summary of planetary life."

Fletcher had been reading the screen. "Here's Chrystal's analysis of the one he brought up."

They studied the elements and primary compounds of a Stryzkal Monitor's constitution.

"Nothing of commercial interest," said Fletcher.

Damon was absorbed in a personal chain of thought. "Did Chrystal actually go down and trap a monitor?"

"That's right. In the water bug. He spent lots of time underwater."

"Everybody to his own methods," said Damon shortly.

Fletcher dropped the cards back in the file. "Whether you like him or not, he's a good field man. Give the devil his due."

"It seems to me that the field phase is over and done with," muttered Damon. "We've got the production line set up; it's a full-time job trying to increase the yield. Of course I may be wrong."

Fletcher laughed, slapped Damon on the skinny shoulder. "I'm not finding fault, Gene. The plain fact is that there're too many avenues for one man to explore. We could keep four men busy."

"Four men?" said Damon. "A dozen is more like it. Three different protoplasmic phases on Sabria, to the single carbon group on Earth! Even Stryzkal only scratched the surface!"

He watched Fletcher for a while, then asked curiously: "What are you after now?"

Fletcher was once more running through the index. "What I came in here to check. The dekabrachs."

Damon leaned back in his chair. "Dekabrachs? Why?"

"There're lots of things about Sabria we don't know,"

114

said Fletcher mildly. "Have you ever been down to look at a dekabrach colony?"

Damon compressed his mouth. "No. I certainly haven't."

Fletcher dialed for the dekabrach card.

It snapped out of the file into the viewer. The screen showed Stryzkal's original photo-drawing, which in many ways conveyed more information than the color stereos. The specimen depicted was something over six feet long, with a pale seallike body terminating in three propulsive vanes. At the head radiated the ten arms from which the creature derived its name—flexible members eighteen inches long, surrounding the black disk which Stryzkal assumed to be an eye.

Fletcher skimmed through the rather sketchy account of the creature's habitat, diet, reproductive methods, and protoplasmic classification. He frowned in dissatisfaction. "There's not much information here—considering that they're one of the more important species. Let's look at the anatomy."

The dekabrach's skeleton was based on an anterior dome of bone, three flexible cartilaginous vertebra, each terminating in a propulsive vane.

The information on the card came to an end. "I thought you said Chrystal made observations on the dekabrachs," growled Damon.

"So he did."

"If he's such a howling good field man, where're his data?"

Fletcher grinned. "Don't blame me, I just work here." He put the card through the screen again.

Under General Comments, Stryzkal had noted, "Dekabrachs appear to belong in the Sabrian Class A group, the silico-carbo-nitride phase, although they deviate in important respects." He had added a few lines of speculation regarding dekabrach relationships to other Sabrian species.

Chrystal merely made the comment, "Checked for commercial application; no specific recommendation."

Fletcher made no comment.

"How closely did he check?" asked Damon.

"In his usual spectacular way. He went down in the

water bug, harpooned one of them, dragged it to the laboratory. Spent three days dissecting it."

"Precious little he's noted here," grumbled Damon. "If I worked three days on a new species like the dekabrachs, I could write a book."

They watched the information repeat itself.

Damon stabbed out with his long bony finger. "Look! That's been blanked over. See those black triangles in the margin? Cancellation marks!"

Fletcher rubbed his chin. "Stranger and stranger."

"It's downright mischievous," Damon cried indignantly, "erasing material without indicating motive or correction."

Fletcher nodded slowly. "It looks like somebody's going to have to consult Chrystal." He considered. "Well—why not now?" He descended to the office, called the Pelagic Recoveries raft.

Chrystal himself appeared on the screen. He was a large blond man with a blooming pink skin and an affable innocence that camouflaged the directness of his mind; his plumpness similarly disguised a powerful musculature. He greeted Fletcher with cautious heartiness, "How's it going on Bio-Minerals? Sometimes I wish I were back with you fellows—this working on your own isn't all it's cracked up to be."

"We've had an accident over here," said Fletcher. "I thought I'd better pass on a warning."

"Accident?" Chrystal looked anxious. "What's happened?"

"Carl Raight took the barge out—and never came back."

Chrystal was shocked. "That's terrible! How . . . why—"

"Apparently something pulled him in. I think it was a monitor mollusk—Stryzkal's Monitor."

Chrystal's pink face wrinkled in puzzlement. "A monitor? Was the barge over shallow water? But there wouldn't be water that shallow. I don't get it."

"I don't either."

Chrystal twisted a cube of white metal between his fin-

116

gers. "That's certainly strange. Raight must be—dead?"

Fletcher nodded somberly. "That's the presumption. I've warned everybody here not to go out alone; I thought I'd better do the same for you."

"That's decent of you, Sam." Chrystal frowned, looked at the cube of metal, put it down. "There's never been trouble on Sabria before."

"I saw dekabrachs under the barge. They might be involved somehow."

Chrystal looked blank. "Dekabrachs? They're harmless enough."

Fletcher nodded noncommittally. "Incidentally, I tried to check on dekabrachs in the micro-library. There wasn't much information. Quite a bit of material has been cancelled out."

Chrystal raised his pale eyebrows. "Why tell me?"

"Because you might have done the cancelling."

Chrystal looked aggrieved. "Now, why should I do something like that? I worked hard for Bio-Minerals, Sam—you know that as well as I do. Now I'm trying to make money for myself. It's no bed of roses, I'll tell you." He touched the cube of white metal, then noticing Fletcher's eyes on it, pushed it to the side of his desk, against Cosey's *Universal Handbook of Constants and Physical Relationships*.

After a pause Fletcher asked, "Well, did you or didn't you blank out part of the dekabrach story?"

Crystal frowned in deep thought. "I might have canceled one or two ideas that turned out bad—nothing very important. I have a hazy idea that I pulled them out of the bank."

"Just what were those ideas?" Fletcher asked in a sardonic voice.

"I don't remember offhand. Something about feeding habits, probably. I suspected that the deks ingested plankton, but that doesn't seem to be the case."

"No?"

"They browse on underwater fungus that grows on the coral banks. That's my best guess."

"Is that all you cut out?"

"I can't think of anything more."

117

Fletcher's eyes went back to the cube of metal. He noticed that it covered the handbook title from the angle of the V in "Universal" to the center of the O in "of." "What's that you've got on your desk, Chrystal? Interesting yourself in metallurgy?"

"No, no," said Chrystal. He picked up the cube, looked at it critically. "Just a bit of alloy. I'm checking it for resistance to reagents. Well, thanks for calling, Sam."

"You don't have any personal ideas on how Raight got it?"

Chrystal looked surprised. "Why on earth do you ask me?"

"You know more about the dekabrachs than anyone else on Sabria."

"I'm afraid I can't help you, Sam."

Fletcher nodded. "Good night."

"Good night, Sam."

Fletcher sat looking at the blank screen. Monitor mollusks—dekabrachs—the blanked microfilm. There was a drift here whose direction he could not identify. The dekabrachs seemed to be involved, and by association, Chrystal. Fletcher put no credence in Chrystal's protestations; he suspected that Chrystal lied as a matter of policy, on almost any subject. Fletcher's mind went to the cube of metal. Chrystal had seemed rather too casual, too quick to brush the matter aside. Fletcher brought out his own *Handbook*. He measured the distance between the fork of the V and the center of the O: 4.9 centimeters. Now, if the block represented a kilogram mass, as was likely with such sample blocks—Fletcher calculated. In a cube, 4.9 centimeters on a side, were 119 cc. Hypothesizing a mass of 1000 grams, the density worked out to 8.4 grams per cc.

Fletcher looked at the figure. In itself it was not particularly suggestive. It might be one of a hundred alloys. There was no point in going too far on a string of hypotheses—still, he looked in the *Handbook*. Nickel, 8.6 grams per cc. Cobalt, 8.7 grams per cc. Noibium, 8.4 grams per cc.

Fletcher sat back, considered. Niobium? An element costly and tedious to synthesize, with limited natural

118

sources and an unsatisfied market. The idea was stimulating. Had Chrystal developed a biological source of niobium? If so, his fortune was made.

Fletcher relaxed in his chair. He felt done in—mentally and physically. His mind went to Carl Raight. He pictured the body drifting loose and haphazard through the night, sinking through miles of water into places where light would never reach. Why had Carl Raight been pillaged of life?

Fletcher began to ache with anger and frustration, at the futility, the indignity of Raight's passing. Carl Raight was too good a man to be dragged to his death into the dark ocean of Sabria.

Fletcher jerked himself upright, marched out of the office, up the steps to the laboratory.

Damon was still busy with his routine work. He had three projects underway: two involving the sequestering of platinum by species of Sabrian algae; the third an attempt to increase the rhenium absorption of an Alphard-Alpha flat-sponge. In each case his basic technique was the same: subjecting succeeding generations to an increasing concentration of metallic salt, under conditions favoring mutation. Certain of the organisms would eventually begin to make functional use of the metal; they would be isolated and transferred to Sabrian brine. A few might survive the shock; some might adapt to the new conditions and begin to absorb the now necessary element.

By selective breeding the desirable qualities of these latter organisms would be intensified; they would then be cultivated on a large-scale basis and the inexhaustible Sabrian waters would soon be made to yield another product.

Coming into the lab, Fletcher found Damon arranging trays of algae cultures in geometrically exact lines. He looked rather sourly over his shoulder at Fletcher.

"I talked to Chrystal," said Fletcher.

Damon became interested. "What did he say?"

"He says he might have wiped a few bad guesses off the film."

"Ridiculous," snapped Damon.

Fletcher went to the table, looked thoughtfully along

119

the row of algae cultures. "Have you run into any niobium on Sabria, Gene?"

"Niobium? No. Not in any appreciable concentration. There are traces in the ocean, naturally. I believe one of the corals shows a set of niobium lines." He cocked his head with birdlike inquisitiveness. "Why do you ask?"

"Just an idea, wild and random."

"I don't suppose Chrystal gave you any satisfaction?"

"None at all."

"Then what's the next move?"

Fletcher hitched himself up on the table. "I'm not sure. There's not much I can do. Unless——" he hesitated.

"Unless what?"

"Unless I make an underwater survey myself."

Damon was appalled. "What do you hope to gain by that?"

Fletcher smiled. "If I knew, I wouldn't need to go. Remember, Chrystal went down, then came back up and stripped the microfile."

"I realize that," said Damon. "Still, I think it's rather . . . well, foolhardy, after what's happened."

"Perhaps, perhaps not." Fletcher slid off the table to the deck. "I'll let it ride till tomorrow, anyway."

He left Damon making out his daily check sheet, descended to the main deck.

Blue Murphy was waiting at the foot of the stairs. Fletcher said, "Well, Murphy?"

The round red face displayed a puzzled frown. "Agostino up there with you?"

Fletcher stopped short. "No."

"He should have relieved me half an hour ago. He's not in the dormitory; he's not in the mess hall."

"Good God," said Fletcher, "another one?"

Murphy looked over his shoulder at the ocean. "They saw him about an hour ago in the mess hall."

"Come on," said Fletcher. "Let's search the raft."

They looked everywhere—processing house, the cupola on the mast, all the nooks and crannies a man might take it into his head to explore. The barges were all at dock;

the launch and catamaran swung at their moorings; the helicopter hulked on the deck with drooping blades.

Agostino was nowhere aboard the raft. No one knew where Agostino had gone; no one knew exactly when he had left.

The crew of the raft collected in the mess hall, making small nervous motions, looking out the portholes over the ocean.

Fletcher could think of very little to say. "Whatever is after us—and we don't know what it is—it can surprise us, and it's watching. We've got to be careful—more than careful!"

Murphy pounded his fist softly on the table. "But what can we do? We can't just stand around like silly cows!"

"Sabria is theoretically a safe planet," said Damon. "According to Stryzkal and the Galactic Index, there are no hostile life forms here."

Murphy snorted, "I wish old Stryzkal was here now to tell me."

"He might be able to theorize back Raight and Agostino." Dave Jones looked at the calendar. "A month to go."

"We'll only run one shift," said Fletcher, "until we get replacements."

"Call them reinforcements," muttered Mahlberg.

"Tomorrow," said Fletcher, "I'm going to take the water bug down, look around, and get an idea what's going on. In the meantime, everybody better carry hatchets or cleavers."

There was soft sound on the windows, on the deck outside. "Rain," said Mahlberg. He looked at the clock on the wall. "Midnight."

The rain hissed through the air, drummed on the walls; the decks ran with water and the masthead lights glared through the slanting streaks.

Fletcher went to the streaming windows, looked toward the process house. "I guess we'd better button up for the night. There's no reason to—" he squinted through the window, then ran to the door and out into the rain.

Water pelted onto his face; he could see very little but the glare of the lights in the rain. And a hint of white along the shining gray-black of the deck, like an old white plastic hose.

A snatch at his ankles; his feet were yanked from under him. He fell flat upon the streaming metal.

Behind him came the thud of feet; there were excited curses, a clang and scrape; the grip on Fletcher's ankles loosened.

Fletcher jumped up, staggered back against the mast. "Something's in the process house," he yelled.

The men pounded off through the rain; Fletcher came after.

But there was nothing in the process house. The doors were wide; the rooms were bright. The squat pulverizers stood on either hand; behind were the pressure tanks, the vats, the pipes of six different colors.

Fletcher pulled the master switch; the hum and grind of the machinery died. "Let's lock up and get back to the dormitory."

Morning was the reverse of evening; first the green gloom of Atreus, warming to pink as Geidion rose behind the clouds. It was a blustery day, with squalls trailing dark curtains all around the compass.

Fletcher ate breakfast, dressed in a skin-tight coverall threaded with heating filaments, then a waterproof garment with a plastic head dome.

The water bug hung on davits at the east edge of the raft, a shell of transparent plastic with the pumps sealed in a metal cell amidships. Submerging, the hull filled with water through valves, which then closed; the bug could submerge to four hundred feet, the hull resisting about half the pressure, the enclosed water the rest. The effect on the passenger was pressure of two hundred feet— safely short of depth delirium.

Fletcher lowered himself into the cockpit; Murphy connected the hoses from the air tanks to Fletcher's helmet, then screwed the port shut. Mahlberg and Hans Heinz winged out the davits. Murphy went to stand by the hoist control. For a moment he hesitated, looking from the dark, pink-dappled water to Fletcher and back at the water.

Fletcher waved his hand. "Lower away." His voice

came from the loudspeaker on the bulkhead behind them.

Murphy swung the handle. The bug eased down. Water gushed in through the valves, up around Fletcher's body, over his head. Bubbles rose from the helmet exhaust valve.

Fletcher tested the pumps, then cast off the grapples. The bug slanted down into the water.

Murphy sighed. "He's got more nerve than I'm ever likely to have."

"He can get away from whatever's after him," said Damon. "He might well be safer than we are here on the raft."

Murphy clapped him on the shoulder. "Damon, my lad—you can climb. Up on top of the mast you'll be safe; it's unlikely that they'll come there to tug you into the water." Murphy raised his eyes to the cupola a hundred feet over the deck. "And I think that's where I'd take myself—if only someone would bring me my food."

Heinz pointed to the water. "There go the bubbles. He went under the raft. Now he's headed north."

The day became stormy. Spume blew over the raft, and it meant a drenching to venture out on deck. The clouds thinned enough to show the outlines of Geidion and Atreus, a blood-orange and a lime.

Suddenly the winds died; the ocean flattened into an uneasy calm. The crew sat in the mess hall drinking coffee, talking in staccato, uneasy voices.

Damon became restless and went up to his laboratory. He came running back down into the mess hall.

"Dekabrachs—they're under the raft! I saw them from the observation deck!"

Murphy shrugged. "They're safe from me."

"I'd like to get hold of one," said Damon. "Alive."

"Don't we have enough trouble already?" growled Dave Jones.

Damon explained patiently. "We know nothing about dekabrachs. They're a highly developed species. Chrystal destroyed all the data we had, and I should have at least one specimen."

Murphy rose to his feet. "I suppose we can scoop one up in a net."

"Good," said Damon. "I'll set up the big tank to receive it."

The crew went out on deck where the weather had turned sultry. The ocean was flat and oily; haze blurred sea and sky together in a smooth gradation of color, from dirty scarlet near the raft to pale pink overhead.

The boom was winged out; a parachute net was attached and lowered quietly into the water. Heinz stood by the winch; Murphy leaned over the rail, staring intently down into the water.

A pale shape drifted out from under the raft. "Lift!" bawled Murphy.

The line snapped taut; the net rose out of the water in a cascade of spray. In the center a six-foot dekabrach pulsed and thrashed, gill slits rasping for water.

The boom swung inboard; the net tripped; the dekabrach slid into the plastic tank.

It darted forward and backward; the plastic dented and bulged where it struck. Then it floated quiet in the center, head-tentacles folded back against the torso.

All hands crowded around the tank. The black eye spot looked back through the transparent walls.

Murphy asked Damon, "Now what?"

"I'd like the tank lifted to the deck outside the laboratory where I can get at it."

"No sooner said than done."

The tank was hoisted and swung to the spot Damon had indicated; Damon went excitedly off to plan his research.

The crew watched the dekabrach for ten or fifteen minutes, then drifted back to the mess hall.

Time passed. Gusts of wind raked up the ocean into a sharp, steep chop. At two o'clock the loudspeaker hissed; the crew stiffened, raised their heads.

Fletcher's voice came from the diaphragm. "Hello, aboard the raft. I'm about two miles northwest. Stand by to haul me aboard."

"*Hah!*" cried Murphy, grinning. "He made it."

"I gave odds against him of four to one," Mahlberg said. "I'm lucky nobody took them."

"Get a move on; he'll be alongside before we're ready."

The crew trooped out to the landing. The water bug came sliding over the ocean, its glistening back riding the dark disorder of the waters.

It slipped quietly up to the raft; grapples clamped to the plates fore and aft. The winch whined, the bug lifted from the water, draining its ballast of water.

Fletcher, in the cockpit, looked tense and tired. He climbed stiffly out of the bug, stretched, unzipped the waterproof suit, pulled off the helmet.

"Well, I'm back." He looked around the group. "Surprised?"

"I'd have lost money on you," Mahlberg told him.

"What did you find out?" asked Damon. "Anything?"

Fletcher nodded. "Plenty. Let me get into clean clothes. I'm wringing wet—sweat." He stopped short, looking up at the tank on the laboratory deck. "When did that come aboard?"

"We netted it about noon," said Murphy. "Damon wanted to look one over."

Fletcher stood looking up at the tank with his shoulders drooping.

"Something wrong?" asked Damon.

"No," said Fletcher. "We couldn't have it worse than it is already." He turned away toward the dormitory.

The crew waited for him in the mess hall; twenty minutes later he appeared. He drew himself a cup of coffee, sat down.

"Well," said Fletcher, "I can't be sure—but it looks as if we're in trouble."

"Dekabrachs?" asked Murphy.

Fletcher nodded.

"I knew it!" Murphy cried in triumph. "You can tell by looking at the blatherskites they're up to no good."

Damon frowned, disapproving of emotional judgments. "Just what is the situation?" he asked Fletcher. "At least, as it appears to you?"

Fletcher chose his words carefully. "Things are going on that we've been unaware of. In the first place, the dekabrachs are socially organized."

"You mean to say—they're intelligent?"

125

Fletcher shook his head. "I don't know for sure. It's possible. It's equally possible that they live by instinct, like social insects."

"How in the world—" began Damon; Fletcher held up a hand. "I'll tell you just what happened; you can ask all the questions you like afterwards." He drank his coffee.

"When I went down under, naturally I was on the alert and kept my eyes peeled. I felt safe enough in the water bug—but funny things have been happening, and I was a little nervous.

"As soon as I was in the water I saw the deka-brachs—five or six of them." Fletcher paused, sipped his coffee.

"What were they doing?" asked Damon.

"Nothing very much. Drifting near a big monitor which had attached itself to the seaweed. The arm was hanging down like a rope—clear out of sight. I edged the bug in just to see what the deks would do; they began backing away. I didn't want to waste too much time under the raft, so I swung off north, toward the Deeps. Halfway there I saw an odd thing; in fact I passed it, and swung around to take another look.

"There were about a dozen deks. They had a monitor—and this one was really big. A giant. It was hanging on a set of balloons or bubbles—some kind of pods that kept it floating, and the deks were easing it along. In this direction."

"In this direction, eh?" mused Murphy.

"What did you do?" asked Manners.

"Well, perhaps it was all an innocent outing—but I didn't want to take any chances. The arm of this monitor would be like a hawser. I turned the bug at the bubbles, burst some, scattered the rest. The monitor dropped like a stone. The deks took off in different directions. I figured I'd won that round. I kept on going north, and pretty soon I came to where the slope starts down into the Deeps. I'd been traveling about twenty feet under; now I lowered to two hundred. I had to turn on the lights, of course—this red twilight doesn't penetrate water too well." Fletcher took another gulp of coffee.

"All the way across the Shallows I'd been passing over coral banks and dodging forests of kelp. Where the shelf slopes down to the Deeps the coral gets to be something fantastic—I suppose there's more water movement, more nourishment, more oxygen. It grows a hundred feet high, in spires and towers, umbrellas, platforms, arches—white pale blue, pale green.

"I came to the edge of a cliff. It was a shock—one minute my lights were on the coral, all these white towers and pinnacles—then there was nothing. I was over the Deeps. I got a little nervous." Fletcher grinned. "Irrational, of course. I checked the fathometer—bottom was twelve thousand feet down. I still didn't like it, and turned around, swung back. Then I noticed lights off to my right. I turned my own off, moved in to investigate. The lights spread out as if I were flying over a city—and that's just about what it was."

"Dekabrachs?" asked Damon.

Fletcher nodded. "Dekabrachs."

"You mean—they built it themselves? Lights and all?"

Fletcher frowned. "That's what I can't be sure of. The coral had grown into shapes that gave them little cubicles to swim in and out of, and do whatever they'd want to do in a house. Certainly they don't need protection from the rain. They hadn't built these coral grottoes in the sense that we build a house—but it didn't look like natural coral either. It's as if they made the coral grow to suit them."

Murphy said doubtfully, "Then they're intelligent."

"No, not necessarily. After all, wasps build complicated nests with no more equipment than a set of instincts."

"What's your opinion?" asked Damon. "Just what impression does it give?"

Fletcher shook his head. "I can't be sure. I don't know what kind of standards to apply. 'Intelligence' is a word that means lots of different things, and the way we generally use it is artificial and specialized."

"I don't get you," said Murphy. "Do you mean these deks are intelligent or don't you?"

Fletcher laughed. "Are men intelligent?"

"Sure. So they say, at least."

127

"Well, what I'm trying to get across is that we can't use man's intelligence as a measure of the dekabrach's mind. We've got to judge him by a different set of values—dekabrach values. Men use tools of metal, ceramic, fiber: inorganic stuff—at least, dead. I can imagine a civilization dependent upon living tools—specialized creatures the master group uses for special purposes. Suppose the dekabrachs live on this basis? They force the coral to grow in the shape they want. They use the monitors for derricks or hoists, or snares, or to grab at something in the upper air."

"Apparently, then," said Damon, "you believe that the dekabrachs are intelligent."

Fletcher shook his head. "Intelligence is just a word—a matter of definition. What the deks do may not be susceptible to human definition."

"It's beyond me," said Murphy, settling back in his chair.

Damon pressed the subject. "I am not a metaphysicist or a semanticist. But it seems that we might apply, or try to apply, a crucial test."

"What difference does it make one way or the other?" asked Murphy.

Fletcher said, "It makes a big difference where the law is concerned."

"Ah," said Murphy, "the Doctrine of Responsibility."

Fletcher nodded. "We could be yanked off the planet for injuring or killing intelligent autochthons. It's been done."

"That's right," said Murphy. "I was on Alkaid Two when Graviton Corporation got in that kind of trouble."

"So if the deks are intelligent, we've got to watch our step. That's why I looked twice when I saw the dek in the tank."

"Well—are they or aren't they?" asked Mahlberg.

"There's one crucial test," Damon repeated.

The crew looked at him expectantly.

"Well?" asked Murphy. "Spill it."

"Communication."

Murphy nodded thoughtfully. "That seems to make sense." He looked at Fletcher. "Did you notice them communicating?"

128

Fletcher shook his head. "Tomorrow I'll take a camera out, and a sound recorder. Then we'll know for sure."

"Incidentally," said Damon, "why were you asking about niobium?"

Fletcher had almost forgotten. "Chrystal had a chunk on his desk. Or maybe he did—I'm not sure."

Damon nodded. "Well, it may be a coincidence, but the deks are loaded with it."

Fletcher stared.

"It's in their blood, and there's a strong concentration in the interior organs."

Fletcher sat with his cup halfway to his mouth. "Enough to make a profit on?"

Damon nodded. "Probably a hundred grams or more in the organism."

"Well, well," said Fletcher. "That's very interesting indeed."

Rain roared down during the night; a great wind came up, lifting and driving the rain and spume. Most of the crew had gone to bed: all except Dave Jones the steward and Manners the radioman, who sat up over a chessboard.

A new sound rose over wind and rain—a metallic groaning, a creaking discord that presently became too loud to ignore. Manners jumped to his feet, went to the window.

"The mast!"

Dimly it could be seen through the rain, swaying like a reed, the arc of oscillation increasing with each swing.

"What can we do?" cried Jones.

One set of guy lines snapped. "Nothing now."

"I'll call Fletcher." Jones ran for the passage to the dormitory.

The mast gave a sudden jerk, poised long seconds at an unlikely angle, then toppled across the process house.

Fletcher appeared, stared out the window. With the masthead light no longer shining down, the raft was dark and ominous. Fletcher shrugged, turned away. "There's nothing we can do tonight. It's worth a man's life to go out on that deck."

In the morning, examination of the wreckage revealed that two of the guy lines had been sawed or clipped cleanly through. The mast, of lightweight construction, was quickly cut apart, and the twisted segments dragged to a corner of the deck. The raft seemed bald and flat.

"Someone or something," said Fletcher, "is anxious to give us as much trouble as possible." He looked across the leaden-pink ocean to where the Pelagic Recoveries raft floated beyond the range of vision.

"Apparently," said Damon, "you refer to Chrystal."

"I have suspicions."

Damon glanced out across the water. "I'm practically certain."

"Suspicion isn't proof," said Fletcher. "In the first place, what would Chrystal hope to gain by attacking us?"

"What would the dekabrachs gain?"

"I don't know," said Fletcher. "I'd like to find out." He went to dress himself in the submarine suit.

The water bug was made ready. Fletcher plugged a camera into the external mounting, connected a sound recorder to a sensitive diaphragm in the skin. He seated himself, pulled the blister over his head.

The water bug was lowered into the ocean. It filled with water, and its glistening back disappeared under the surface.

The crew patched the roof of the process house, jury-rigged an antenna.

The day passed; twilight came, and plum-colored evening.

The loudspeaker hissed and sputtered. Fletcher's voice, tired and tense, said, "Stand by; I'm coming in."

The crew gathered by the rail, straining their eyes through the dusk.

One of the dully glistening wave fronts held its shape, drew closer, and became the water bug.

The grapples were dropped; the water bug drained its ballast and was hoisted into the chocks.

Fletcher jumped down to the deck, leaned limply against one of the davits. "I've had enough submerging to last me a while."

"What did you find out?" Damon asked anxiously.

"I've got it all on film. I'll run it off as soon as my head stops ringing."

Fletcher took a hot shower, then came down to the mess hall and ate the bowl of stew Jones put in front of him, while Manners transferred the film Fletcher had shot from camera to projector.

"I've made up my mind to two things," said Fletcher. "First—the deks are intelligent. Second, if they communicate with each other, it's by means imperceptible to human beings."

Damon blinked, surprised and dissatisfied. "That's almost a contradiction."

"Just watch," said Fletcher. "You can see for yourself."

Manners started the projector; the screen went bright.

"The first few feet show nothing very much," said Fletcher. "I drove directly out to the end of the shelf and cruised along the edge of the Deeps. It drops away like the end of the world—straight down. I found a big colony about ten miles west of the one I found yesterday—almost a city."

" 'City' implies civilization," Damon asserted in a didactic voice.

Fletcher shrugged. "If civilization means manipulation of environment—somewhere I've heard that definition—they're civilized."

"But they don't communicate?"

"Check the film for yourself."

The screen was dark with the color of the ocean. "I made a circle out over the Deeps," said Fletcher, "turned off my lights, started the camera, and came in slow."

A pale constellation appeared in the center of the screen, separated into a swarm of sparks. They brightened and expanded; behind them appeared the outlines, tall and dim, of coral minarets, towers, spires, and spikes. They defined themselves as Fletcher moved closer. From the screen came Fletcher's recorded voice. "These formations vary in height from fifty to two hundred feet, along a front of about half a mile."

The picture expanded. Black holes showed on the faces

131

of the spires; pale dekabrach shapes swam quietly in and out. "Notice," said the voice, "the area in front of the colony. It seems to be a shelf, or a storage yard. From up here it's hard to see; I'll drop down a hundred feet or so."

The picture changed; the screen darkened. "I'm dropping now—depth meter reads three hundred sixty feet ... Three eighty ... I can't see too well; I hope the camera is getting it all."

Fletcher commented. "You're seeing it better now than I could; the luminous areas in the coral don't shine too strongly down there."

The screen showed the base of the coral structures and a nearly level bench fifty feet wide. The camera took a quick swing, peered down over the verge, into blackness.

"I was curious," said Fletcher. "The shelf didn't look natural. It isn't. Notice the outlines on down? They're just barely perceptible. The shelf is artificial—a terrace, a front porch."

The camera swung back to the bench, which now appeared to be marked off into areas vaguely differentiated in color.

Fletcher's voice said, "Those colored areas are like plots in a garden—there's a different kind of plant, or weed, or animal on each of them. I'll come in closer. Here are monitors." The screen showed two or three dozen heavy hemispheres, then passed on to what appeared to be eels with saw edges along their sides, attached to the bench by suckers. Next were float-bladders, then a great number of black cones with very long, loose tails.

Damon said in a puzzled voice, "What keeps them there?"

"You'll have to ask the dekabrachs," said Fletcher.

"I would if I knew how."

"I still haven't seen them do anything intelligent," said Murphy.

"Watch," said Fletcher.

Into the field of vision swam a pair of dekabrachs, black eye spots staring out of the screen at the men in the mess hall.

"Dekabrachs," came Fletcher's voice from the screen.

"Up to now, I don't think they noticed me," Fletcher

132

himself commented. "I carried no lights, and made no contrast against the background. Perhaps they felt the pump."

The dekabrachs turned together, dropped sharply for the shelf.

"Notice," said Fletcher, "they saw a problem, and the same solution occurred to both at the same time. There was no communication."

The dekabrachs had diminished to pale blurs on one of the dark areas along the shelf.

"I didn't know what was happening," said Fletcher, "but I decided to move. And then—the camera doesn't show this—I felt bumps on the hull, as if someone were throwing rocks. I couldn't see what was going on until something hit the dome right in front of my face. It was a little torpedo, with a long nose like a knitting needle. I took off fast, before the deks tried something else."

The screen went black. Fletcher's voice said, "I'm out over the Deeps, running parallel with the edge of the Shallows." Indeterminate shapes swam across the screen, pale wisps blurred by watery distance. "I came back along the edge of the shelf," said Fletcher, "and found the colony I saw yesterday."

Once more the screen showed spires, tall structures, pale blue, pale green, ivory. "I'm going in close," came Fletcher's voice. "I'm going to look in one of those holes." The towers expanded; ahead was a dark hole.

"Right here I turned on the nose-light," said Fletcher. The black hole suddenly became a bright cylindrical chamber fifteen feet deep. The walls were lined with glistening colored globes, like Christmas-tree ornaments. A dekabrach floated in the center of the chamber. Translucent tendrils ending in knobs extended from the chamber walls and seemed to be punching and kneading the seal-smooth hide.

"I don't know what's going on," said Fletcher, "but the dek doesn't like me looking in on him."

The dekabrach backed to the rear of the chamber; the knobbed tendrils jerked away, into the walls.

"I looked into the next hole."

Another black hole became a bright chamber as the

133

searchlight burnt in. A dekabrach floated quietly, holding a sphere of pink jelly before its eye. The wall-tendrils were not to be seen.

"This one didn't move," said Fletcher. "He was asleep or hypnotized or too scared. I started to take off—and there was the most awful thump. I thought I was a goner."

The screen gave a great lurch. Something dark hurtled past and into the depths.

"I looked up," said Fletcher. "I couldn't see anything but about a dozen deks. Apparently they'd floated a big rock over me and dropped it. I started the pump and headed for home."

The screen went blank.

Damon was impressed. "I agree that they show patterns of intelligent behavior. Did you detect any sounds?"

"Nothing. I had the recorder going all the time. Not a vibration other than the bumps on the hull."

Damon's face was wry with dissatisfaction. "They must communicate somehow—how could they get along otherwise?"

"Not unless they're telepathic," said Fletcher. "I watched carefully. They make no sounds or motions to each other—none at all."

Manners asked, "Could they possibly radiate radio waves? Or infrared?"

Damon said glumly, "The one in the tank doesn't."

"Oh, come now," said Murphy, "are there no intelligent races that don't communicate?"

"None," said Damon. "They use different methods—sounds, signals, radiation—but all communicate."

"How about telepathy?" Heinz suggested.

"We've never come up against it; I don't believe we'll find it here," said Damon.

"My personal theory," said Fletcher, "is that they think alike, and don't need to communicate."

Damon shook his head dubiously.

"Assume that they work on a basis of communal empathy," Fletcher went on, "that this is the way they've evolved. Men are individualistic; they need speech. The deks are identical; they're aware of what's going on without words." He reflected a few seconds. "I suppose, in a certain sense, they do communicate. For instance, a dek wants to extend the garden in front of its tower. It possibly waits till another dek comes near, then carries out a rock—indicating what it wants to do."

"Communication by example," said Damon.

"That's right—if you can call it communication. It permits a measure of cooperation—but clearly no small talk, no planning for the future or traditions of the past."

"Perhaps not even awareness of past or future; perhaps no awareness of time!" cried Damon.

"It's hard to estimate their native intelligence. It might be remarkably high, or it might be low; the lack of communication must be a terrific handicap."

"Handicap or not," said Mahlberg, "they've certainly got us on the run."

"And why?" cried Murphy, pounding the table with his big red fist. "That's the question. We've never bothered them. And all of a sudden, Raight's gone, and Agostino. Also our mast. Who knows what they'll think of tonight? Why? That's what I want to know."

"That," said Fletcher, "is a question I'm going to put to Ted Chrystal tomorrow."

Fletcher dressed himself in clean blue twill, ate a silent breakfast, and went out to the flight deck.

Murphy and Mahlberg had thrown the guy lines off the helicopter and wiped the dome clean of salt film.

Fletcher climbed into the cabin, twisted the inspection knob. Green light—everything in order.

Murphy said half-hopefully, "Maybe I'd better come with you, Sam—if there's any chance of trouble."

"Trouble? Why should there be trouble?"

"I wouldn't put much past Chrystal."

"I wouldn't either," said Fletcher. "But—there won't be any trouble."

He started the blades. The ram-tubes caught hold; the copter lifted, slanted up, away from the raft, and off into the northeast. Bio-Minerals became a bright tablet on the irregular wad of seaweed.

The day was dull, brooding, windless, apparently build-

135

ing up for one of the tremendous electrical storms which came every few weeks. Fletcher accelerated, thinking to get his errand over with as soon as possible.

Miles of ocean slid past; Pelagic Recoveries appeared ahead.

Twenty miles southwest from the raft, Fletcher overtook a small barge laden with raw material for Chrystal's macerators and leaching columns; he noticed that there were two men aboard, both huddled inside the plastic canopy. Pelagic Recoveries perhaps had its troubles too, thought Fletcher.

Chrystal's raft was little different from Bio-Minerals', except that the mast still rose from the central deck and there was activity in the process house. They had not shut down, whatever their troubles.

Fletcher landed on the flight deck. As he stopped the blades, Chrystal came out of the office—a big blond man with a round jocular face.

Fletcher jumped down to the deck. "Hello, Ted," he said in a guarded voice.

Chrystal approached with cheerful smile. "Hello, Sam! Long time since we've seen you." He shook hands briskly. "What's new at Bio-Minerals? Certainly too bad about Carl."

"That's what I want to talk about." Fletcher looked around the deck. Two of the crew stood watching. "Can we go to your office?"

"Sure, by all means." Chrystal led the way to the office, slid back the door. "Here we are."

Fletcher entered the office. Chrystal walked behind his desk. "Have a seat." He sat down in his own chair. "Now—what's on your mind? But first, how about a drink? You like Scotch, as I recall."

"Not today, thanks." Fletcher shifted in his chair. "Ted, we're up against a serious problem here on Sabria, and we might as well talk plainly about it."

"Certainly," said Chrystal. "Go right ahead."

"Carl Raight's dead. And Agostino."

Chrystal's eyebrows rose in shock. "Agostino too? How?"

136

"We don't know. He just disappeared."

Chrystal took a moment to digest the information. Then he shook his head in perplexity. "I can't understand it. We've never had trouble like this before."

"Nothing happening over here?"

Chrystal frowned. "Well—nothing to speak of. Your call put us on our guard."

"The dekabrachs seem to be responsible."

Chrystal blinked and pursed his lips, but said nothing.

"Have you been going out after dekabrachs, Ted?"

"Well now, Sam—" Chrystal hesitated, drumming his fingers on the desk. "That's hardly a fair question. Even if we were working with dekabrachs—or polyps or club-moss or wire-eels—I don't think I'd want to say, one way or the other."

"I'm not interested in your business secrets," said Fletcher. "The point is this: the deks appear to be an intelligent species. I have reason to believe that you're processing them for their niobium content. Apparently they're doing their best to retaliate and don't care whom they hurt. They've killed two of our men. I've got a right to know what's going on."

Chrystal nodded. "I can understand your viewpoint—but I don't follow your chain of reasoning. For instance, you told me that a monitor had done for Raight. Now you say dekabrach. Also, what leads you to believe I'm going for niobium?"

"Let's not try to kid each other, Ted."

Chrystal looked shocked, then annoyed.

"When you were still working for Bio-Minerals," Fletcher went on, "you discovered that the deks were full of niobium. You wiped all that information out of the files, got financial backing, built this raft. Since then you've been hauling in dekabrachs."

Chrystal leaned back, surveyed Fletcher coolly. "Aren't you jumping to conclusions?"

"If I am, all you've got to do is deny it."

"Your attitude isn't very pleasant, Sam."

"I didn't come here to be pleasant. We've lost two men; also our mast. We've had to shut down."

"I'm sorry to hear that—" began Chrystal.

Fletcher interrupted: "So far, Chrystal, I've given you the benefit of the doubt."

Chrystal was surprised. "How so?"

"I'm assuming you didn't know the deks were intelligent, that they're protected by the Responsibility Act."

"Well?"

"Now you know. You don't have the excuse of ignorance."

Chrystal was silent for a few seconds. "Well, Sam—these are all rather astonishing statements."

"Do you deny them?"

"Of course I do!" said Chrystal with a flash of spirit.

"And you're not processing dekabrach?"

"Easy now. After all, Sam, this is my raft. You can't come aboard and chase me back and forth. It's high time you understood it."

Fletcher drew himself a little away, as if Chrystal's mere proximity were unpleasant.

"You're not giving me a plain answer."

Chrystal leaned back in his chair, put his fingers together, puffed out his cheeks. "I don't intend to."

The barge that Fletcher had passed on his way was edging close to the raft. Fletcher watched it work against the mooring stage, snap its grapples. He asked, "What's on that barge?"

"Frankly, it's none of your business."

Fletcher rose to his feet, went to the window. Chrystal made uneasy protesting noises. Fletcher ignored him. The two barge handlers had not emerged from the control cabin. They seemed to be waiting for a gangway which was being swung into position by the cargo boom.

Fletcher watched in growing curiosity and puzzlement. The gangway was built like a trough with high plywood walls.

He turned to Chrystal. "What's going on out there?"

Chrystal was chewing his lower lip, rather red in the face. "Sam, you came storming over here, making wild accusations, calling me dirty names—by implication—and I don't say a word. I try to allow for the strain you're under; I value the good will between our two outfits. I'll

138

show you some documents that will prove once and for all—" he sorted through a sheaf of miscellaneous pamphlets.

Fletcher stood by the window, with half an eye for Chrystal, half for what was occurring out on deck.

The gangway was dropped into position; the barge handlers were ready to disembark.

Fletcher decided to see what was going on. He started for the door.

Chrystal's face went stiff and cold. "Sam, I'm warning you, don't go out there!"

"Why not?"

"Because I say so."

Fletcher slid open the door; Chrystal made a motion to jump up from his chair; then he slowly sank back.

Fletcher walked out the door, crossed the deck toward the barge.

A man in the process house saw him through the window and made urgent gestures.

Fletcher hesitated, then turned to look at the barge. A couple of more steps and he could look into the hold. He stepped forward, craned his neck. From the corner of his eye he saw the gestures becoming frantic. The man disappeared from the window.

The hold was full of limp white dekabrachs.

"Get back, you fool!" came a yell from the process house.

Perhaps a faint sound warned Fletcher; instead of backing away, he threw himself to the deck. A small object flipped over his head from the direction of the ocean, with a peculiar fluttering buzz. It struck a bullhead, dropped—a fishlike torpedo, with a long needlelike proboscis. It came flapping toward Fletcher, who rose to his feet and ran crouching and dodging back toward the office.

Two more of the fishlike darts missed him by inches; Fletcher hurled himself through the door into the office.

Chrystal had not moved from the desk. Fletcher went panting up to him. "Pity I didn't get stuck, isn't it?"

"I warned you not to go out there."

139

Fletcher turned to look across the deck. The barge handlers ran down the troughlike gangway to the process house. A glittering school of dart-fish flickered up out of the water, struck at the plywood.

Fletcher turned back to Chrystal. "I saw dekabrachs in that barge. Hundreds of them."

Chrystal had regained whatever composure he had lost. "Well? What if there are?"

"You know they're intelligent as well as I do."

Chrystal smiled, shook his head.

Fletcher's temper was going raw. "You're ruining Sabria for all of us!"

Chrystal held up his hand. "Easy, Sam. Fish are fish."

"Not when they're intelligent and kill men in retaliation."

Chrystal wagged his head. "*Are* they intelligent?"

Fletcher waited until he could control his voice. "Yes. They are."

Chrystal reasoned with him. "How do you know they are? Have you talked with them?"

"Naturally I haven't talked with them."

"They display a few social patterns. So do seals."

Fletcher came up closer, glared down at Chrystal. "I'm not going to argue definitions with you. I want you to stop hunting dekabrach, because you're endangering lives aboard both our rafts."

Chrystal leaned back a trifle. "Now, Sam, you know you can't intimidate me."

"You've killed two men; I've escaped by inches three times now. I'm not running that kind of risk to put money in your pocket."

"You're jumping to conclusions," Chrystal protested. "In the first place you've never proved—"

"I've proved enough! You've got to stop, that's all there is to it!"

Chrystal slowly shook his head. "I don't see how you're going to stop me, Sam." He brought his hand up from under the desk; it held a small gun. "Nobody's going to bulldoze me, not on my own raft."

Fletcher reacted instantly, taking Chrystal by surprise. He grabbed Chrystal's wrist, banged it against the angle

140

of the desk. The gun flashed, seared a groove in the desk, fell from Chrystal's limp fingers to the floor. Chrystal hissed and cursed, bent to recover it, but Fletcher leaped over the desk, pushed him over backward in his chair. On the way Chrystal kicked at Fletcher's face, caught him a glancing blow on the cheek that sent Fletcher to his knees.

Both men dived for the gun; Fletcher reached it first, rose to his feet, backed to the wall. "Now we know where we stand."

"Put down that gun!"

Fletcher shook his head. "I'm putting you under arrest—civilian arrest. You're coming to Bio-Minerals until the inspector arrives."

Chrystal seemed dumfounded. "What?"

"I said I'm taking you to the Bio-Minerals raft. The inspector is due in three weeks, and I'll turn you over to him."

"You're crazy, Fletcher."

"Perhaps. But I'm taking no chances with you." Fletcher motioned with the gun. "Get going. Out to the copter."

Chrystal coolly folded his arms. "I'm not going to move. You can't scare me by waving a gun."

Fletcher raised his arm, sighted, pulled the trigger. The jet of fire grazed Chrystal's rump. Chrystal jumped, clapped his hand to the scorch.

"Next shot will be somewhat closer," said Fletcher.

Chrystal glared like a boar from a thicket. "You realize I can bring kidnapping charges against you?"

"I'm not kidnapping you. I'm placing you under arrest."

"I'll sue Bio-Minerals for everything they've got."

"Unless Bio-Minerals sues you first. Get going!"

The entire crew met the helicopter: Damon, Blue Murphy, Manners, Hans Heinz, Mahlberg, and Dave Jones.

Chrystal jumped haughtily to the deck, surveyed the men with whom he had once worked. "I've got something to say to you men."

The crew watched him silently.

Chrystal jerked his thumb at Fletcher. "Sam's got himself in a peck of trouble. I told him I'm going to throw the book at him and that's what I'm going to do." He looked from face to face. If you men help him, you'll be accessories. I advise you, take that gun away from him and fly me back to my raft."

He looked around the circle, but met only coolness and hostility. He shrugged angrily. "Very well, you'll be liable for the same penalties as Fletcher. Kidnapping is a serious crime, don't forget."

Murphy asked Fletcher, "What shall we do with the varmint?"

"Put him in Carl's room; that's the best place for him. Come on, Chrystal."

Back in the mess hall, after locking the door on Chrystal, Fletcher told the crew, "I don't need to tell you—be careful of Chrystal. He's tricky. Don't talk to him. Don't run any errands of any kind. Call me if he wants anything. Everybody got that straight?"

Damon asked dubiously, "Aren't we getting in rather deep water?"

"Do you have an alternative suggestion?" asked Fletcher. "I'm certainly willing to listen."

Damon thought. "Wouldn't he agree to stop hunting dekabrach?"

"No. He refused point-blank."

"Well," said Damon reluctantly, "I guess we're doing the right thing. But we've got to prove a criminal charge. The inspector won't care whether or not Chrystal's cheated Bio-Minerals."

Fletcher said, "If there's any backfire on this, I'll take full responsibility."

"Nonsense," said Murphy. "We're all in this together. I say you did just right. In fact, we ought to hand the sculpin over to the deks, and see what they'd say to him."

After a few minutes Fletcher and Damon went up to the laboratory to look at the captive dekabrach. It floated quietly in the center of the tank, the ten arms at right angles to its body, the black eye area staring through the glass.

"If it's intelligent," said Fletcher, "it must be as interested in us as we are in it."

"I'm not so sure it's intelligent," said Damon stubbornly. "Why doesn't it try to communicate?"

"I hope the inspector doesn't think along the same lines," said Fletcher. "After all, we don't have an airtight case against Chrystal."

Damon looked worried. "Bevington isn't a very imaginative man. In fact, he's rather official in his outlook."

Fletcher and the dekabrach examined each other. "I know it's intelligent—but how can I prove it?"

"If it's intelligent," Damon insisted doggedly, "it can communicate."

"If it can't," said Fletcher, "then it's our move."

"What do you mean?"

"We'll have to teach it."

Damon's expression became so perplexed and worried that Fletcher broke into laughter.

"I don't see what's funny," Damon complained. "After all, what you propose is . . . well, it's unprecedented."

"I suppose it is," said Fletcher. "But it's got to be done, nevertheless. How's your linguistic background?"

"Very limited."

"Mine is even more so."

They stood looking at the dekabrach.

"Don't forget," said Damon, "we've got to keep it alive. That means, we've got to feed it." He gave Fletcher a caustic glance. "I suppose you'll admit it eats."

"I know for sure it doesn't live by photosynthesis," said Fletcher. "There's just not enough light. I believe Chrystal mentioned on the microfilm that it ate coral fungus. Just a minute." He started for the door.

"Where are you going?"

"To check with Chrystal. He's certainly noted their stomach contents."

"He won't tell you," Damon said at Fletcher's back.

Fletcher returned ten minutes later.

"Well?" asked Damon in a skeptical voice.

Fletcher looked pleased with himself. "Coral fungus mostly. Bits of tender young kelp shoots, stylax worms, sea-oranges."

"Chrystal told you all this?" asked Damon incredulously.

"That's right. I explained to him that he and the dekabrach were both our guests, that we planned to treat them exactly alike. If the dekabrach ate well, so would Chrystal. That was all he needed."

Later, Fletcher and Damon stood in the laboratory watching the dekabrach ingest black-green balls of fungus.

"Two days," said Damon sourly, "and what have we accomplished? Nothing."

Fletcher was less pessimistic. "We've made progress in a negative sense. We're pretty sure it has no auditory apparatus, that it doesn't react to sound, and apparently lacks means for making sound. Therefore, we've got to use visual methods to make contact."

"I envy you your optimism," Damon declared. "The beast has given no grounds to suspect either the capacity or the desire for communication."

"Patience," said Fletcher. "It still probably doesn't know what we're trying to do, and probably fears the worst."

"We not only have to teach it a language," grumbled Damon, "we've got to introduce it to the idea that communication is possible. And then invent a language."

Fletcher grinned. "Let's get to work."

"Certainly," said Damon. "But how?"

They inspected the dekabrach, and the black eye area stared back through the wall of the tank. "We've got to work out a set of visual conventions," said Fletcher. "The ten arms are its most sensitive organs, and presumably are controlled by the most highly organized section of its brain. So—we work out a set of signals based on the dek's arm movements."

"Does that give us enough scope?"

"I should think so. The arms are flexible tubes of muscle. They can assume at least five distinct positions; straight forward, diagonal forward, perpendicular, diagonal back, and straight back. Since the beast has ten arms,

144

evidently there are ten to the fifth power combinations—a hundred thousand."

"Certainly adequate."

"It's our job to work out syntax and vocabulary—a little difficult for an engineer and a biochemist, but have a go at it."

Damon was becoming interested in the project. "It's merely a matter of consistency and sound basic structure. If the dek's got any comprehension whatever, we'll put it across."

"If we don't," said Fletcher. "we're gone geese—and Chrystal winds up taking over the Bio-Minerals raft."

They seated themselves at the laboratory table.

"We have to assume that the deks have no language," said Fletcher.

Damon grumbled uncertainly, and ran his fingers through his hair in annoyed confusion. "Not proven. Frankly, I don't think it's even likely. We can argue back and forth about whether they *could* get along on communal empathy, and such like—but that's a couple of light-years from answering the question whether they *do*.

"They *could* be using telepathy, as we said; they could also be emitting modulated X-rays, establishing long-and-short code signals in some unknown-to-us subspace, hyperspace, or interspace—they *could* be doing almost anything we never heard of.

"As I see it, our best bet—and best hope—is that they *do* have some form of encoding system by which they communicate among themselves. Obviously, as you know, they have to have an internal coding-and-communication system; that's what a neuromuscular structure, with feedback loops, is. Any complex organism has to have communication internally. The whole point of this requirement of language as a means of classifying alien life forms is to distinguish between true communities of individual thinking entities, and the communal insect type of apparent intelligence.

"Now *if* they've got an ant- or bee-like city over there, we're sunk, and Chrystal wins. You can't teach an ant to talk; the nest-group has intelligence, but the individual doesn't.

145

"So we've got to assume they do have a language—or, to be more general, a formalized encoding system for intercommunication.

"We can also assume it uses a pathway not available to our organisms. That sound sensible to you?"

Fletcher nodded. "Call it a working hypothesis, anyway. We know we haven't seen any indication the dek has tried to signal us."

"Which suggests the creature is not intelligent."

Fletcher ignored the comment. "If we knew more about their habits, emotions, attitudes, we'd have a better framework for this new language."

"It seems placid enough."

The dekabrach moved its arms back and forth idly. The visual-surface studied the two men.

"Well," said Fletcher with a sigh, "first a system of notation." He brought forward a model of the dekabrach's head, which Manners had constructed. The arms were of flexible conduit, and could be bent into various positions. "We number the arms 0 to 9 around the clock, starting with this one here at the top. The five positions—forward, diagonal forward, erect, diagonal back, and back—we call A, B, K, X, Y. K is normal position, and when an arm is at K, it won't be noted."

Damon nodded his agreement. "That's sound enough."

"The logical first step would seem to be numbers."

Together they worked out a system of numeration, and constructed a chart:

The colon (:) indicates a composite signal: i. e. two or more separate signals.

Number	0	1	2	et cetera
Signal	OY	1Y	2Y	et cetera
	10	11	12	et cetera
	OY, 1Y	OY, 1Y: 1Y	OY, 1Y: 2Y	et cetera / et cetera
	20	21	22	et cetera
	OY, 2Y	OY, 2Y: 1Y	OY, 2Y: 2Y	et cetera / et cetera
	100	101	102	et cetera
	OX, 1Y	OX, 1Y: 1Y	OX, 1Y: 2Y	et cetera / et cetera
	110	111	112	et cetera
	OX, 1Y: OY, 1Y	OX, 1Y: OY, 1Y: 1Y	OX, 1Y: OY, 1Y: 2Y	et cetera / et cetera / et cetera
	120	121	122	et cetera
	OX, 1Y: OY, 2Y	OX, 1Y: OY, 2Y: 1Y	OX, 1Y: OY, 2Y: 2Y	et cetera / et cetera / et cetera
	200	201	202	et cetera
	OX, 2Y			et cetera
	1000			et cetera
	OB, 1Y			et cetera
	2000			et cetera
	OB, 2Y			et cetera

Damon said, "It's consistent—but possibly cumbersome; for instance, to indicate five thousand seven hundred sixty-six, it's necessary to make the signal . . . let's see: OB, 5Y, then OX, 7Y, then OY, 6Y, then 6Y."

"Don't forget that these are signals, not vocalizations," said Fletcher. "Even so, it's no more cumbersome than 'five thousand, seven hundred sixty-six.' "

"I suppose you're right."

"Now—words."

Damon leaned back in his chair. "We just can't build a vocabulary and call it a language."

"I wish I knew more linguistic theory," said Fletcher. "Naturally, we won't go into any abstractions."

"Our basic English structure might be a good idea," Damon mused, "with English parts of speech. That is, nouns are things, adjectives are attributes of things, verbs are the displacements which things undergo, or the absence of displacement."

Fletcher reflected. "We could simplify even further, to nouns, verbs and verbal modifiers."

"Is that feasible? How, for instance, would you say 'the large raft'?"

"We'd use a verb meaning 'to grow big'. 'Raft expanded'. Something like that."

"Humph," grumbled Damon. "You don't envisage a very expressive language."

"I don't see why it shouldn't be. Presumably the deks will modify whatever we give them to suit their own needs. If we get across just a basic set of ideas, they'll take it from there. Or by that time someone'll be out here who knows what he's doing."

"O.K.," said Damon. "Get on with your Basic Dekabrach."

"First, let's list the ideas a dek would find useful and familiar."

"I'll take the nouns," said Damon. "You take the verbs; you can also have your modifiers." He wrote. "No. 1: water."

After considerable discussion and modification, a sparse list of basic nouns and verbs was agreed upon, and assigned signals.

The simulated dekabrach head was arranged before the tank, with a series of lights on a board nearby to represent numbers.

"With a coding machine we could simply type out our message," said Damon. "The machine would dictate the impulses to the arms of the model."

Fletcher agreed. "Fine, if we had the equipment and several weeks to tinker around with it. Too bad we don't. Now—let's start. The numbers first. You work the lights, I'll move the arms. Just one to nine for now."

Several hours passed. The dekabrach floated quietly, the black eye spot observing.

Feeding time approached. Damon displayed the black-green fungus balls; Fletcher arranged the signal for "food" on the arms of the model. A few morsels were dropped into the tank.

The dekabrach quietly sucked them into its oral tube.

148

Damon went through the pantomime of offering food to the model. Fletcher moved the arms to the signal "food." Damon ostentatiously placed the fungus ball in the model's oral tube, then faced the tank, and offered food to the dekabrach.

The dekabrach watched impassively.

Two weeks passed. Fletcher went up to Raight's old room to talk to Chrystal, whom he found reading a book from the microfilm library.

Chrystal extinguished the image of the book, swung his legs over the side of the bed, sat up.

Fletcher said, "In a very few days the inspector is due."

"So?"

"It's occurred to me that you might have made an honest mistake. At least I can see the possibility."

"Thanks," said Chrystal, "for nothing."

"I don't want to victimize you on what may be an honest mistake."

"Thanks again—but what do you want?"

"If you'll cooperate with me in having dekabrachs recognized as an intelligent life form, I won't press charges against you."

Chrystal raised his eyebrows. "That's big of you. And I'm supposed to keep my complaints to myself?"

"If the deks are intelligent, you don't have any complaints."

Chrystal looked keenly at Fletcher. "You don't sound too happy. The dek won't talk, eh?" Chrystal laughed at his joke.

Fletcher restrained his annoyance. "We're working on him."

"But you're beginning to suspect he's not so intelligent as you thought."

Fletcher turned to go. "This one only knows fourteen signals so far. But it's learning two or three a day."

"Hey!" called Chrystal. "Wait a minute!"

Fletcher stopped at the door. "What for?"

"I don't believe you."

"That's your privilege."

"Let me see this dek make signals."

149

Fletcher shook his head. "You're better off in here."

Chrystal glared. "Isn't that a rather unreasonable attitude?"

"I hope not." He looked around the room. "Anything you're lacking?"

"No." Chrystal turned the switch, and his book flashed once more on the ceiling.

Fletcher left the room; the door closed behind him; the bolts shot home. Chrystal sat up alertly, jumped to his feet with a peculiar lightness, went to the door, listened.

Fletcher's footfalls diminished down the corridor. Chrystal returned to the bed in two strides, reached under the pillow, brought out a length of electric cord, detached from a desk lamp. He had adapted two pencils as electrodes, notching through the wood to the lead, binding a wire around the graphite core so exposed. For resistance in the circuit he included a lamp bulb.

He then went to the window. He could see the deck all the way down to the eastern edge of the raft, as well as behind the office to the storage bins at the back of the process house.

The deck was empty. The only movement was a white wisp of steam rising from the circulation flue, and the hurrying pink and scarlet clouds behind.

Chrystal went to work, whistling soundlessly between intently pursed lips. He plugged the cord into the baseboard strip, held the two pencils to the window, struck an arc, burnt at the groove which now ran nearly halfway around the window—the only means by which he could cut through the tempered beryl-silica glass.

It was slow work and very delicate. The arc was weak and fractious; fumes grated in Chrystal's throat. He persevered, blinking through watery eyes, twisting his head this way and that, until five-thirty, half an hour before his evening meal, when he put the equipment away. He dared not work after dark, for fear the flicker of light would arouse suspicion.

The days passed. Each morning Geidion and Atreus brought their respective flushes of scarlet and pale green

150

to the dull sky; each evening they vanished in sad dark sunsets behind the western ocean.

A makeshift antenna had been jury-rigged from the top of the laboratory to a pole over the living quarters. Early one afternoon Manners blew the general alarm in short jubilant blasts to announce a signal from the LG-19, putting into Sabria on its regular six-months call. Tomorrow evening lighters would swing down from orbit, bringing the sector inspector, supplies, and new crews for both Bio-Minerals and Pelagic Recoveries.

Bottles were broken out in the mess hall; there was loud talk, brave plans, laughter.

Exactly on schedule the lighters—four of them—burst through the clouds. Two settled into the ocean beside Bio-Minerals, two more dropped down to the Pelagic Recoveries raft.

Lines were carried out by the launch, the lighters were warped against the dock.

First aboard the raft was Inspector Bevington, a brisk little man, immaculate in his dark-blue and white uniform. He represented the government, interpreted its multiplicity of rules, laws, and ordinances; he was empowered to adjudicate minor offenses, take custody of criminals, investigate violations of galactic law, check living conditions and safety practices, collect imposts, bonds and duties, and, in general, personify the government in all of its faces and phases.

The job might well have invited graft and petty tyranny, were not the inspectors themselves subject to minute inspection.

Bevington was considered the most conscientious and the most humorless man in the service. If he was not particularly liked, he was at least respected.

Fletcher met him at the edge of the raft. Bevington glanced at him sharply, wondering why Fletcher was grinning so broadly. Fletcher was thinking that now would be a dramatic moment for one of the dekabrach's monitors to reach up out of the sea and clutch Bevington's ankle. But there was no disturbance; Bevington leaped to the raft without interference.

151

He shook hands with Fletcher, seeking up and down the dock. "Where's Mr. Raight?"

Fletcher was taken aback; he had become accustomed to Raight's absence. "Why—he's dead."

It was Bevington's turn to be startled. "Dead?"

"Come along to the office," said Fletcher, "and I'll tell you about it. This last has been a wild month." He looked up to the window of Raight's old room where he expected to see Chrystal looking down. But the window was empty. Fletcher halted. Empty indeed! The window was vacant even of glass! He started down the deck.

"Here!" cried Bevington. "Where are you going?"

Fletcher paused long enough to call over his shoulder, "You'd better come with me!" then ran to the door leading into the mess hall. Bevington came after him, frowning in annoyance and surprise.

Fletcher looked into the mess hall, hesitated, came back out on deck, looked up at the vacant window. Where was Chrystal? As he had not come along the deck at the front of the raft, he must have headed for the process house.

"This way," said Fletcher.

"Just a minute!" protested Bevington. "I want to know just what and where—"

But Fletcher was on his way down the eastern side of the raft toward the process house, where the lighter crew was already looking over the cases of precious metal to be transshipped. They glanced up when Fletcher and Bevington came running up.

"Did anybody just come past?" asked Fletcher. "A big blond fellow?"

"He went in there." The lightermen pointed toward the process house.

Fletcher whirled, ran through the doorway. Beside the leaching columns, he found Hans Heinz, looking ruffled and angry.

"Chrystal come through here?" Fletcher panted.

"Did he come through here! Like a hurricane. He gave me a push in the face."

"Where did he go?"

Heinz pointed. "Out on the front deck."

Fletcher and Bevington ran off, Bevington demanding petulantly, "Exactly what's going on here?"

"I'll explain in a minute," yelled Fletcher. He ran out on deck, looked toward the barges and launch.

No Ted Chrystal.

He could only have gone in one direction: back toward the living quarters, having led Fletcher and Bevington in a complete circle.

A sudden thought hit Fletcher. "The helicopter!"

But the helicopter stood undisturbed, with its guy lines taut. Murphy came toward them, looking perplexedly over his shoulder.

"Seen Chrystal?" asked Fletcher.

Murphy pointed. "He just went up them steps."

"The laboratory!" cried Fletcher in sudden agony. Heart in his mouth he pounded up the steps, Murphy and Bevington at his heels. If only Damon were in the laboratory, not down on the dock or in the mess hall.

The lab was empty—except for the tank with the dekabrach.

The water was cloudy, bluish. The dekabrach was thrashing from end to end of the tank, the ten arms kinked and knotted.

Fletcher jumped on a table, vaulted directly into the tank. He wrapped his arms around the writhing body, lifted. The supple shape squirmed out of his grasp. Fletcher grabbed again, heaved in desperation, raised it out of the tank.

"Grab hold," he hissed to Murphy between clenched teeth. "Lay it on the table."

Damon came rushing in. "What's going on?"

"Poison," said Fletcher. "Give Murphy a hand."

Damon and Murphy managed to lay the dekabrach on the table. Fletcher barked, "Stand back, flood coming!" He slid the clamps from the side of the tank, the flexible plastic collapsed; a thousand gallons of water gushed across the floor.

Fletcher's skin was beginning to burn. "Acid! Damon, get a bucket, wash off the dek. Keep him wet."

The circulatory system was still pumping brine into the

tank. Fletcher tore off his trousers, which held the acid against his skin, gave himself a quick rinse, turned the brine-pipe around the tank, flushing off the acid.

The dekabrach lay limp, its propulsion vanes twitching. Fletcher felt sick and dull. "Try sodium carbonate," he told Damon. "Maybe we can neutralize some of the acid." On sudden thought he turned to Murphy, "Go get Chrystal. Don't let him get away."

This was the moment that Chrystal chose to stroll into the laboratory. He looked around the room in mild surprise, hopped up on a chair to avoid the water.

"What's going on in here?"

Fletcher said grimly, "You'll find out." To Murphy: "Don't let him get away."

"Murderer!" cried Damon in a voice that broke with strain and grief.

Chrystal raised his eyebrows in shock. "Murderer?"

Bevington looked back and forth between Fletcher, Chrystal, and Damon. "Murderer? What's all this?"

"Just what the law specifies," said Fletcher. "Knowingly and willfully destroying one of an intelligent species. Murder."

The tank was rinsed; he clamped up the sides. The fresh brine began to rise up the sides.

"Now," said Fletcher, "hoist the dek back in."

Damon shook his head hopelessly. "He's done for. He's not moving."

"We'll put him back in anyway," said Fletcher.

"I'd like to put Chrystal in there with him," Damon said with passionate bitterness.

"Come now," Bevington reproved him, "let's have no more talk like that. I don't know what's going on, but I don't like anything of what I hear."

Chrystal, looking amused and aloof, said, "I don't know what's going on either."

They lifted the dekabrach, lowered him into the tank.

The water was about six inches deep, rising too slowly to suit Fletcher.

"Oxygen," he called. Damon ran to the locker. Fletcher looked at Chrystal. "So you don't know what I'm talking about?"

"Your pet fish dies; don't try to pin it on me."

Damon handed Fletcher a breather-tube from the oxygen tank; Fletcher thrust it into the water beside the dekabrach's gills. Oxygen bubbled up; Fletcher agitated the water, urged it into the gill openings. The water was nine inches deep. "Sodium carbonate," Fletcher said over his shoulder. "Enough to neutralize what's left of the acid."

Bevington asked in an uncertain voice, "Is it going to live?"

"I don't know."

Bevington squinted sideways at Chrystal, who shook his head. "Don't blame me."

The water rose. The dekabrach's arms lay limp, floating in all directions like Medusa locks.

Fletcher rubbed the sweat off his forehead. "If only I knew what to do! I can't give it a shot of brandy; I'd probably poison it."

The arms began to stiffen, extend. "Ah," breathed Fletcher, "that's better." He beckoned to Damon. "Gene, take over here—keep the oxygen going into the gills." He jumped to the floor where Murphy was flushing the floor with buckets of water.

Chrystal was talking with great earnestness to Bevington. "I've gone in fear of my life these last three weeks! Fletcher is an absolute madman; you'd better send up for a doctor—or a psychiatrist." He caught Fletcher's eye, paused. Fletcher came slowly across the room. Chrystal returned to the inspector, whose expression was harassed and uneasy.

"I'm registering an official complaint," said Chrystal. "Against Bio-Minerals in general and Sam Fletcher in particular. As a representative of the law, I insist that you place Fletcher under arrest for criminal offenses against my person."

"Well," said Bevington, cautiously glancing at Fletcher, "I'll certainly make an investigation."

"He kidnapped me at the point of a gun," cried Chrystal. "He's kept me locked up for three weeks!"

"To keep you from murdering the dekabrachs," said Fletcher.

"That's the second time you've said that," Chrystal remarked ominously. "Bevington is a witness. You're liable for slander."

"Truth isn't slander."

"I've netted dekabrachs, so what? I also cut kelp and net coelocanths. You do the same."

"The deks are intelligent. That makes a difference." Fletcher turned to Bevington. "He knows it as well as I do. He'd process men for the calcium in their bones if he could make money at it!"

"You're a liar!" cried Chrystal.

Bevington held up his hands. "Let's have order here! I can't get to the bottom of this unless someone presents facts."

"He doesn't have facts," Chrystal insisted. "He's trying to run my raft off of Sabria—can't stand the competition!"

Fletcher ignored him. He said to Bevington, "You want facts. That's why the dekabrach is in that tank, and that's why Chrystal poured acid in on him."

"Let's get something straight," said Bevington, giving Chrystal a hard stare. "Did you pour acid into that tank?"

Chrystal folded his arms. "The question is completely ridiculous."

"Did you? No evasions now."

Chrystal hesitated, then said firmly, "No. And there's no vestige of proof that I did so."

Bevington nodded. "I see." He turned to Fletcher. "You spoke of facts. What facts?"

Fletcher went to the tank, where Damon still was swirling oxygenated water into the gills. "How's he coming?"

Damon shook his head dubiously. "He's acting peculiar. I wonder if the acid got him internally?"

Fletcher watched the long pale shape for a half minute. "Well, let's try him. That's all we can do."

He crossed the room, wheeled the model dekabrach forward. Chrystal laughed, turned away in disgust. "What do you plan to demonstrate?" asked Bevington.

"I'm going to show you that the dekabrach is intelligent and is able to communicate."

"Well, well," said Bevington. "This is something new, is it not?"

"Correct." Fletcher arranged his notebook.

"How did you learn his language?"

"It isn't his—it's a code we worked out between us."

Bevington inspected the model, looked down at the notebook. "These are the signals?"

Fletcher explained the system. "He's got a vocabulary of fifty-eight words, not counting numbers up to nine."

"I see." Bevington took a seat. "Go ahead. It's your show."

Chrystal turned. "I don't have to watch this fakery."

Bevington said, "You'd better stay here and protect your interests; if you don't, no one else will."

Fletcher moved the arms of the model. "This is admittedly a crude setup; with time and money we'll work out something better. Now, I'll start with numbers."

Chrystal said contemptuously, "I could train a rabbit to count that way."

"After a minute," said Fletcher, "I'll try something harder. I'll ask who poisoned him."

"Just a minute!" bawled Chrystal. "You can't tie me up that way!"

Bevington reached for the notebook. "How will you ask? What signals do you use?"

Fletcher pointed them out. "First, interrogation. The idea of interrogation is an abstraction which the dek still doesn't completely understand. We've established a convention of choice, or alternation, like, 'which do you want?' Maybe he'll catch on what I'm after."

"Very well—'interrogation.' Then what?"

"Dekabrach—receive—hot—water. ('Hot water' is for acid.) Interrogation: Man—give—hot—water?"

Bevington nodded. "That's fair enough. Go ahead."

Fletcher worked the signals. The black eye area watched. Damon said anxiously, "He's restless—very uneasy."

Fletcher completed the signals. The dekabrach's arms waved once or twice, gave a puzzled jerk.

157

Fletcher repeated the set of signals, added an extra "in-terrogation—man?"

The arms moved slowly. " 'Man'," read Fletcher. Bev-ington nodded. "Man. But which man?"

Fletcher said to Murphy, "Stand in front of the tank." And he signaled, "Man—give—hot—water—interroga-tion."

The dekabrach's arms moved. " 'Null-zero'," read Fletcher. "No. Damon—step in front of the tank." He signaled the dekabrach. "Man—give—hot—water—inter-rogation."

" 'Null'."

Fletcher turned to Bevington. "You stand in front of the tank." He signaled.

" 'Null'."

Everyone looked at Chrystal. "Your turn," said Fletcher. "Step forward, Chrystal."

Chrystal came slowly forward, "I'm not a chump, Fletcher. I can see through your gimmick."

The dekabrach was moving its arms. Fletcher read the signals, Bevington looking over his shoulder at the note-book.

" 'Man—give—hot—water.' "

Chrystal started to protest. Bevington quieted him. "Stand in front of the tank, Chrystal." To Fletcher: "Ask once again."

Fletcher signaled. The dekabrach responded. " 'Man —give—hot—water. Yellow. Man. Sharp. Come. Give —hot—water. Go.' "

There was silence in the laboratory.

"Well," said Bevington flatly, "I think you've made your case, Fletcher."

"You're not going to get me that easy," said Chrystal.

"Quiet," rasped Bevington. "It's clear enough what's happened—"

"It's clear what's going to happen," said Chrystal in a voice husky with rage. He was holding Fletcher's gun. "I secured this before I came up here—and it looks as if—" he raised the gun toward the tank, squinted, his big white hand tightened on the trigger. Fletcher's heart went dead and cold.

"Hey!" shouted Murphy.

Chrystal jerked. Murphy threw his bucket; Chrystal fired at Murphy, missed. Damon jumped at him, Chrystal swung the gun. The white-hot jet pierced Damon's shoulder. Damon, screaming like a hurt horse, wrapped his bony arms around Chrystal. Fletcher and Murphy closed in, wrested away the gun, locked Chrystal's arms behind him.

Bevington said grimly, "You're in trouble now, Chrystal, even if you weren't before."

Fletcher said, "He's killed hundreds and hundreds of the deks. Indirectly he killed Carl Raight and John Agostino. He's got a lot to answer for."

The replacement crew had moved down to the raft from the LG-19. Fletcher, Damon, Murphy, and the rest of the old crew sat in the mess hall, with six months of leisure ahead of them.

Damon's left arm hung in a sling; with his right he fiddled with his coffee cup. "I don't quite know what I'll be doing. I have no plans. The fact is, I'm rather up in the air."

Fletcher went to the window, looked out across the dark scarlet ocean. "I'm staying on."

"What?" cried Murphy. "Did I hear you right?"

Fletcher came back to the table. "I can't understand it myself."

Murphy shook his head in total lack of comprehension. "You can't be serious."

"I'm an engineer, a working man," said Fletcher. "I don't have a lust for power, or any desire to change the universe—but it seems as if Damon and I set something into motion—something important—and I want to see it through."

"You mean, teaching the deks to communicate?"

"That's right. Chrystal attacked them, forced them to protect themselves. He revolutionized their lives. Damon and I revolutionized the life of this one dek in an entirely new way. But we've just started. Think of the potentialities! Imagine a population of men in a fertile land—men like ourselves except that they never learned to talk. Then someone gives them contact with a new uni-

159

verse—an intellectual stimulus like nothing they'd ever experienced. Think of their reactions, their new attack on life! The deks are in that same position—except that we've just started with them. It's anybody's guess what they'll achieve—and somehow, I want to be part of it. Even if I didn't, I couldn't leave with the job half done."

Damon said suddenly, "I think I'll stay on, too."

"You two have gone stir crazy," said Jones. "I can't get away fast enough."

The LG-19 had been gone three weeks; operations had become routine aboard the raft. Shift followed shift; the bins began to fill with new ingots, new blocks of precious metal.

Fletcher and Damon had worked long hours with the dekabrach; today would see the great experiment.

The tank was hoisted to the edge of the dock.

Fletcher signaled once again his final message. "Man show you signals. You bring many dekabrachs, man show signals. Interrogation."

The arms moved in assent. Fletcher backed away; the tank was hoisted, lowered over the side, submerged.

The dekabrach floated up, drifted a moment near the surface, slid down into the dark water.

"There goes Prometheus," said Damon, "bearing the gift of the gods."

"Better call it the gift of gab," said Fletcher grinning.

The pale shape had vanished from sight. "Ten gets you fifty he won't be back," Caldur, the new superintendent, offered them.

"I'm not betting," said Fletcher, "just hoping."

"What will you do if he doesn't come back?"

Fletcher shrugged. "Perhaps net another, teach him. After a while it's bound to take hold."

Three hours went by. Mists began to close in; rains blurred the sky.

Damon, peering over the side, looked up. "I see a dek. But is it our dek?"

A dekabrach came to the surface. It moved its arms. "Many—dekabrachs. Show—signals."

"Professor Damon," said Fletcher, "your first class."